CALL OF THE
SYRENSEA

The Serpentine Throne Book Two

Susan Stradiotto

BRONZEWOOD
BOOKS

Eden Prairie, MN

CALL OF THE SYRENSEA

Published by
Bronzewood Books
14920 Ironwood Ct.
Eden Prairie, MN 55346

Cover & Interior Design: Bronzewood Books

Edited by: Owl Pro Editing

Library of Congress Control Number: _____

Paperback ISBN-13: 978-1-949357-20-2

eBook ISBN-13: 978-1-949357-21-9

Printed in the USA

Dedicated to:

My beautiful daughter Mackenzie, who adored the Tsinti and is a wanderer at heart like her mother and father.

THE NOR
BARR

TAMATORI

THE SYRENSEA

ISE

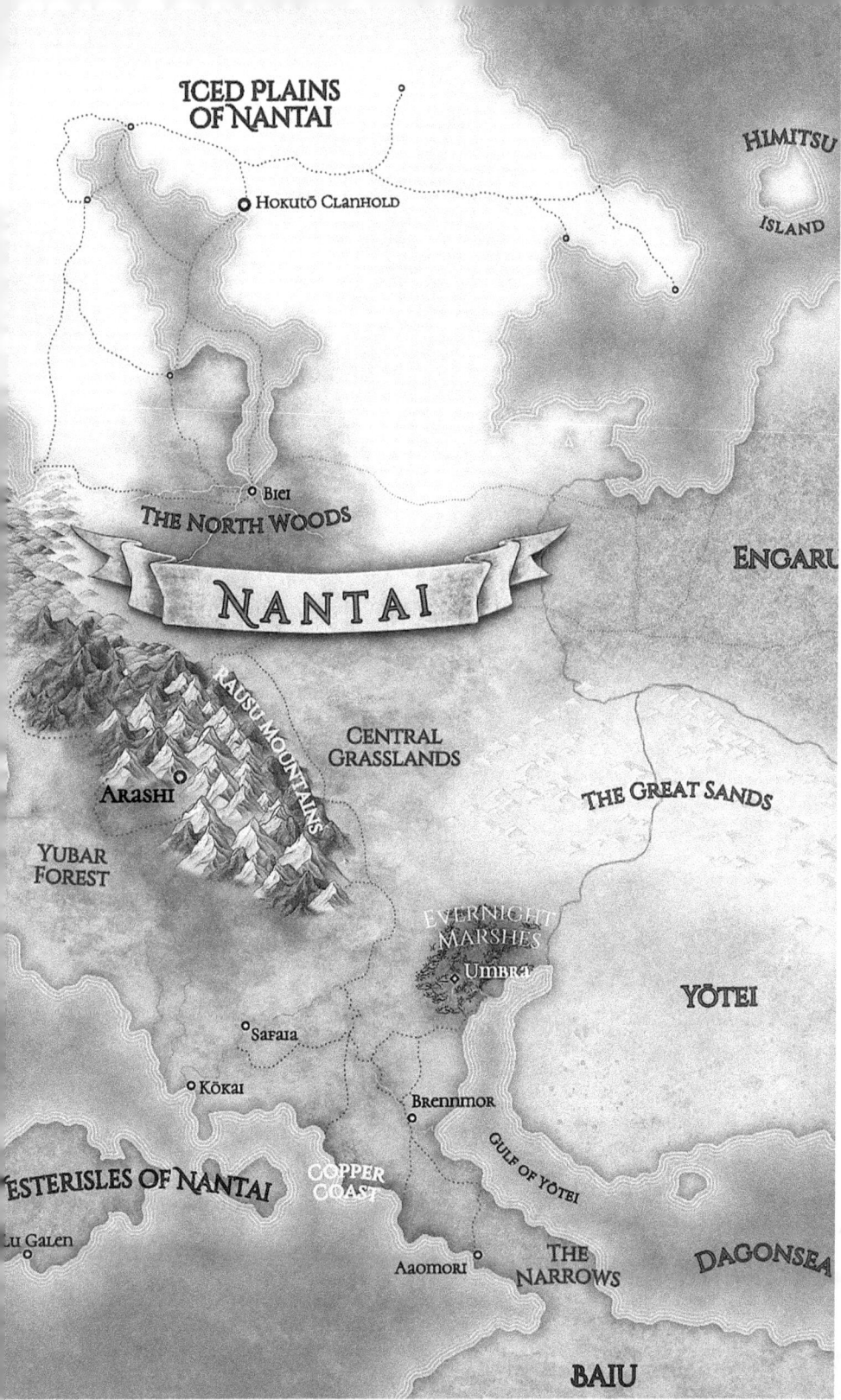

ICED PLAINS OF NANTAI

Hokutō Clanhold

HIMITSU ISLAND

Biei

THE NORTH WOODS

NANTAI

ENGARU

RAUSU MOUNTAINS

CENTRAL GRASSLANDS

THE GREAT SANDS

Arashi

YUBAR FOREST

EVERNIGHT MARSHES

Umbra

YŌTEI

Safaia

Kōkai

Brennmor

GULF OF YŌTEI

ESTERISLES OF NANTAI

COPPER COAST

DAGONSEA

Lu Galen

Aaomori

THE NARROWS

BAIU

ONE

Beyond Arashi, Nantai

MUSCLES BURNED AND BUNCHED within my calves. A pack bounced on my shoulders. Scimityne scabbards thudded against my legs with every step, a new thing I'd accepted from the guard Gaelynne, who had helped us escape. They held weapons Thalaj had crafted specially for me and, as such, something I would treasure always. My skirts rustled over the grasses of the vale, growing heavy and damp with predawn dew. My heart and legs pumped in concert.

Away from all I'd ever known, I ran.

The moon goddess, Selene, neared the end of her watch in the westward skies, but the sun god, Otarr, had yet to brighten the mountainous horizon in the east.

Over my shoulder lay the city of Arashi, the only place I'd truly known in the passing of more than twenty summers. Since the time of Emperor Makenyn five long ages before, it'd been the Nantai's star city at the base of Mount Sundai. Held within Arashi's walls and beside the great waterfalls, Stormskeep Castle—home of the Serpentine Throne and the seat of emperors and empresses throughout the ages—watched over the city and the vale beyond.

Built around Sundai River Falls, Arashi had been where my father, Tennō Atheryn Evangale had ruled before his mysterious disappearance. The castle and city streets were where my sisters and I had played as younglings, learning the limits of our sorcery. Inside those walls, other young Storm Sorcerers and I had gathered in the citadel near the keep to learn from the Havengales— priests of our Holy Triad. Selene's priestess, Tasmynne, had told stories using painted boards to warn us of the dangers beyond Arashi's walls—the winged predators of the Rausu Mountains and the nekodai in the north. Both vicious birds and mammoth cats always thirsted for youthful blood in the tales. Younglings perished under beaks, claws, and fangs. The paintings on the storyboards had always been splattered with crimson blood, and though I'd clung to her stories, nightmares followed.

But for all the learning and despite the stories, I'd never seen the expanse of my country with my own eyes. There were so many people throughout Nantai I'd never met. Now, I ran toward them to find what I had lost— what Nantai had lost.

Father. Emperor.

Within Arashi, I had answered my duties and followed my father's decrees within the annals. Though I would have preferred otherwise, though the stones I wore around my neck called me away from the city, and though I hadn't been wise enough for such a mantle, I had ascended to sit upon the Serpentine Throne. I'd become Empress of Nantai.

Kōgō Mairynne Evangale.

I'd seen my first guard and protector healed after his encounter with the Small Folk of the Evernight Marshes—a mission he'd tended on my behalf. Then, I'd sentenced my best friend's murderer to imprisonment within Stormskeep's spires. But on this morning after decreeing that Aunt Nadialynne Riversgale, my mother's twin sister, ascend to the throne during my absence, I answered the call of the stones I kept on a necklace near my heart. Through the vale, I escaped home and duty with my protector Thalaj in search of Father. Despite my sisters', my advisers', and the clergy's beliefs, within my heart and soul, I had no doubts. Atheryn Evangale, Tennō of Nantai, lived. And the throne rightfully belonged to him.

We ran as morning's twilight came.

With my storm-fed sorcery, I called the wind when I tired. Yet, after a time, my breathing steadied into a quicker rhythm as a renewed wave of energy flowed through my body.

Gloaming lifted.

Night retreated.

Behind us, the citadel's bells began to toll, awakening Arashi for the common daylight routines. Almost to the Yubar Forest at the edge of the vale, Thalaj stretched his step. I struggled to keep pace at his side while counting the gongs in my mind . . . four, five, six. A glance behind revealed sunlight kissing the top of Mount Sundai, setting the mists of the waterfalls aglow, turning Stormskeep's spires golden, then unfolding to cover the castle and the city itself. The stone wall fortifications protecting the city within gleamed under Otarr's light as his rays stretched from them across the valley, like arms brushing the moistened grass. We left a dark trail, but the sooner we reached the woods, the sooner we could more easily cover our tracks. Only moments before Otarr's bright eyes found us, I ducked under a low-hanging branch into the tree cover. Broad leaves and shadow welcomed us into the southernmost swath of the Yubar Forest.

Along with the city and my home, I left my doubts behind. The time for my adventure had come, and with it, the time for me to let go of my imperial duties. Between the city gates and the forest's edge, every step I'd taken had solidified my conviction. I would deliver my father back to his seat upon the Serpentine Throne. It was a new duty, one I had chosen, and a band had released from around my chest. I had to trust in my peoples' traditions and that the decree I'd written would come to pass. Eventually, I would see Arashi again, but whether I'd remain at Stormskeep then and grow into the ruler my father believed me to be remained a worry for another day. This day, I pursued my own will.

Truth to thine self first, my father's voice echoed in my mind.

"Yes, Father," I whispered in agreement and pushed my legs harder.

Ahead, Thalaj stopped under the shade of broad leaves. When I arrived at his side, he relieved me of my pack, unlatched it, and tossed me a tunic and rough-spun pants. "Change. I estimate we have an hour to get as far into the forest as possible before the warnings go up." He turned away, giving me the privacy to do as he bade.

Once I'd dressed in simpler clothing and resecured my pack, we continued deeper into the Yubar Forest, shaded from Otarr's light by the tangled canopy above. We trekked over decaying leaves, frogs croaking in the nearby wetlands along the river. While we'd left behind the roaring of the falls, the Sundai babbled gently and birds sang above. I'd been to the edge of the forest and just inside, but never this far within. Mother and Father hadn't allowed me to venture into its depths, warning that I would easily get lost or carried off by one of the wolf packs rumored to prowl the forest that stretched from the slope of the Rausu Mountains my people called home toward the Syrensea in the west. Aside from the paintings and storyboards, I'd never seen these wolves, and I'd often suspected the Hallowgales had invented the tale to keep younglings from wandering off.

The serenity under the trees allowed me to further contemplate this journey and allow my guard to do the same. I'd given him space thus far because I trusted him implicitly. But the original plan had been for him to go in search of Father with a small team of Storm Sorcerer guards. When the bells began to chime from the citadel again, quieter then as they were farther away, I skip-stepped and caught up to Thalaj, pulling him to a stop. "We're an hour into the forest. Tell me why we're going at this alone," I demanded, my words firm but lacking outrage. I had trouble putting forward a hard empress's façade when I felt a thrill to simply be free.

He slowed his pace but kept us moving. "In the Evernight, I was captured."

"I thought there was a fight, that you and Roryn—"

He shook his head. "I left Roryn in the camp while I went to retrieve the totem."

"You went in alone?" I asked, my eyes wide with surprise that he'd abandoned his only ally on the mission. "Rumor tells the Small Folk feed on our magic."

He nodded. "Aye, I entered alone. Though I am uncertain that bit about the Small Folk feeding on magic

13

is true. I took a beating, but I'm better now." He cocked a half smile.

I shook my head. "I may never understand you, Thalaj Nightingale. You say you trust Roryn but you wouldn't work with him. Instead, you risk your life trying to what?"

He gave me a sidelong glance but refused me a believable answer. "It's simply who and *what* I am . . . how I trained." He stepped over a fallen branch and extended a hand to help me. "My methods are of little importance."

Huffing, I accepted his hand. "Had you perished in the foolish attempt, where would I be now? You are the one responsible for helping me away from Arashi."

He winced but dismissed my accusation. "Regardless of how I entered the marshes, I learned that we not only need to find the Tsinti, but we need to seek out their witch wife. To answer your question about why we left without a larger search party, I didn't believe we would have a hope of gaining entrance into a Tsinti camp if we brought a full traveling party. The Tsinti, themselves, are a private folk, only traveling under a *tsym*. We've spoken of this before. You know that they only reveal themselves to those they choose. It's why I went for the totem."

I fought an urge to reach for my necklace where the stones and the totem hung near my heart. "How will we know where to look?"

"I'm guessing a bit on that one, but they're a nomadic people. Nomads have a pattern, and I believe they will bring the silks from Yōtei in the east to the Southern Fork market in autumn."

My stomach flipped. "We're going to the Great Market?" For years, I'd begged Father to take us with them to the largest market in our lands, where everyone congregated along the southernmost fork of the Betsu River for the time between the two moons of the cooling season to share in news from every corner of Nantai and to trade.

"No. I wouldn't risk taking you into such a place."

I glared. "Why? I'll not trade the confines of Stormskeep for a travel companion who keeps me equally secluded."

The manner in which his look flitted to mine intoned many thoughts, amusement mayhap, but certainly exasperation. He chose to speak none of that. "If that had been my plan, I would have brought the travel party." He looked up at a bird calling above and whistled back. Amused, his eyes settled back on mine. "No. I plan to try to find the Tsinti in the Central Grasslands before they make their way down the Betsu."

"Oh." I slumped.

Thalaj gave a small laugh. "You're empress, Mairynne, and you have your majority now. Once we've concluded this quest, you may attend the market every year, and I will ensure your protection when you do."

We traveled in companionable silence for several minutes, then he added, "My hope is that alone, the Tsinti will welcome us into their caravan."

Otarr must have been high in the sky by the time we stopped by the river to eat. Even under the Yubar's shade, it grew hotter. I'd almost drained my waterskin, and relief struck me hard as we stopped for water. I sat on a boulder beside the babbling stream. Thalaj filled his skein, then reached for mine. As he held it in the clear, flowing waters, I lifted my hair. Holding my other hand forward, palm up, I found the center of my sorcery powers and gathered a breeze from the water surface to cool my face and neck.

Thalaj stood and plugged the cap back into place but then dropped the waterskin as a sound ripped through the sky. I shrank, sliding from my rock. My guard freed his scimitynes with a *schling* breaking the thick silence under the greenery. We both searched above for the source of the bone-chilling screech. While night had obscured the source before, trees did so then. Though after the sound, a rush of wind sent the treetops rustling and a rain of green leaves showered around us. Then . . . all went still once more. Whatever it had been had silenced the sounds of the Yubar. Frogs and birds alike paused.

I didn't breathe for long moments following, but when my guard seemed to release a bit of tension, I looked at him with wide eyes. "That thing. Whatever it is. Does it follow us? Have you heard it any time when we're not together?"

He came out of his crouch and slowly slid his weapons back into their homes. The birds chirped again, tentatively at first. Frogs joined in the chorus, resuming their rhythmic croak. The restored song seemed to signal safety had returned.

"No," Thalaj said simply.

While I'd been so certain of my journey only a couple of hours before, a part of me began to long for the protection of the castle's stone walls. "Should we—"

"No," he cut me off and turned a cold, arresting stare in my direction. "Mairynne, I have no idea what that is, but I'm not going to coddle you on this journey. We'll run into many things, and we'll face them together. If some beast truly follows us, it will eventually have to do more than screech in the sky, and we'll manage the situation when that happens. Until then, it's out of our control."

I hesitated, fingered the warm stone about my neck, and slowly reached to touch the hilt of a *scimityne* at my hip. I stiffened. A resolution formed. Beyond Arashi's walls, I was no longer Lady Mairynne, not Princess, Empress, and certainly not Kōgō. Out here, I was simply Mairynne. A world of new experiences lay before me. Certainly, we'd face new challenges and obstacles, along with all the wonder of Nantai beyond the city where I'd come of age. I could no longer reach for the comfort and safety of all I'd known.

My hand grasping the small, curved sword's hilt, I looked up into Thalaj's dark features with a new wonder. "You'll teach me to use these?"

"Not today." He smiled, obviously reading the change in me. "Not today, but very soon. I will." He gathered my discarded water bladder and handed it to me, also helping me up from my reclined position against the rock. "Before nightfall, I'd like to make it to a small grove that marks the midpoint between Arashi and the edge of the grasslands. Tomorrow, we'll press forward to seek the Tsinti on the Central Grasslands. If they accept us, we'll have their tsym to protect us from sight, and I'll begin showing you the elementary moves."

◇◇◇◇◇◇◇◇

THE REMAINDER OF THE day passed as Thalaj and I hiked around trees, over fallen limbs, and southward. At our right side, the Sundai continued her path toward the Syrensea. A soft bed of decaying leaves cushioned our steps. Under our boots, sticks crackled from time to time, adding to the lullaby of the running water, rustling foliage, and chirping creatures. The light faded, green seemingly growing thicker, as the day moved toward night once again.

"If I am not mistaken, where the river bends just

ahead is the clearing," said Thalaj. He looked toward the bend and up into the leafy ceiling. "Perhaps there will be enough light remaining to catch a fish for an evening meal."

When we broke through the edge of the trees, we saw a clearing reminiscent of the scene from the Cloud Courtier performance of the legend of Sosano and Inara beside the river. Small flowers nestled amid wispy grasses with the last rays of Otarr streaming down. Mist drifted into the clearing, thickening. I wondered what the delicate grasses would look like when morning's dew wept from their blades.

Thalaj dropped his pack at the trunk of a large tree and said, "Aahhh, yes. A blessed fog," seeming relieved of a worry I couldn't fathom. When I looked at him questioningly, he answered, "It will provide cover enough that a fire won't be visible from afar. Gaelynne and Roryn were to send the Arashi guards farther west, toward the North Sundai, but if any other search party has picked up our trail, the mist should help keep us out of sight."

He gathered dry sticks and fallen limbs from beneath the trees and stacked them carefully, then stood and placed his hands on his hips above his weapon belt, some hidden thoughts alive in his mind as he regarded me.

"It is disquieting when you look at me so," I said, dancing around asking directly what he thought. Thalaj had been a fixture in Stormskeep, always near and watching over our family. He had been young when he came to Arashi and dedicated himself to my father. To this day, I am uncertain he'd gained his majority at the time he joined the Arashi guard. I'd been younger still. Mayhap it had been Father's direction to watch over me, but from the beginning we shared an easy, comfortable friendship. Only in the times nearing my mother's death had a hint of something more begun to surface. This would be the first of many nights where we'd be alone together. My purpose out here had little to do with Thalaj, but I couldn't think of another person I'd prefer to have at my side. Despite that I wished for more connection, there was naught suggestive in the purse of his lips as he considered.

In an instant, he grinned boyishly. "How would you like to learn to catch a fish?"

I wrinkled my nose at first, then changed my mind and shrugged. Anywhere beyond a city, the skill might be of use. And I had no inkling of when I might return to the city. The taller grass blades tickled my palm as I crossed toward Thalaj and the forest. He squatted, retrieved a line from his pack, and grabbed a thinner, greener stick from those he'd collected and tested how it bent. When he seemed satisfied, he tilted his head toward the river and began walking. I left my pack with his beside our camp at the clearing and followed him back toward the Sundai. Upon the banks, Thalaj passed me the line and stick, then crouched again, removed his boots, and rolled his breeches to his knees. With bare feet, Thalaj stepped into the shallow waters. He hissed. The waters flowing from Mount Sundai were colder than even he—as half Frost Fighter—had expected. Dipping his hands into the shallow water, he reached deeper several times and then stood with a tiny fish writhing between his fingers. From his belt, he produced a barbed piece of metal.

I winced when he stabbed it through the baby fish, regretful for the small animal's fate. I said a quick prayer to Atun for the life given so that we might hunt for our next meal.

Thalaj took the end of the line from me and tied it around the metal. As he tied the other end of the line to the stick, he nodded to my boots. "You'll want to take those off to keep them dry."

With my legs bare too, I joined him in the water. Indeed, it was icy upon my feet and ankles, and I entered much slower than my guard.

As I reached his side, he handed me the wider end of the stick and pointed. "See the dark pool there? That's where the fish will be." He made motion as if he still held the stick. "Swing the stick and aim the line there."

I tried once, but got the barb snagged in my breeches. Laughter—a rare thing from Thalaj—surrounded us as he freed my inadvertent catch. Afterward, he demonstrated a better technique. When the line settled between us and the dark pool he'd mentioned, he handed the stick back to me.

"What now?" I asked.

He folded his arms over his chest and answered, "We wait."

In a matter of moments, the stick started jiggling in my hands.

"Oh . . . oh . . . oh, what do I do?" I stammered.

"Pull back."

I did.

It jerked and pulled.

"Good. Now just hold." He reached for the line, swiping twice before he captured it and pulled. It took several tries, but he wrestled a fish the size of his forearm out of the water. "To the shore," he barked, already moving in that direction.

I hurried over, my eyes wide and curious.

With the silvery fish lying in the grass and gaping to breathe, Thalaj pulled the barb from its mouth, removed the smaller fish, and tucked the metal back into his belt. I snarled as he reached a finger inside the fish's mouth and lifted it. "Well done, for your first time," he teased.

Near camp, the fog had thickened while we fished. Thalaj cleaned the scales from the fish and swiped his knife along the bones, pulling away chunks of white meat. The light was near gone as he handed the skewered meat to me and built a fire. The fish, smoky from the fire, near melted on my tongue. Afterward, we sat shoulder to shoulder watching the flames die down. Autumn and cooler days would soon be upon us, but that night still felt warm.

Eventually, Thalaj offered me a blanket upon which to sleep and spread out his own.

I stood and once again imitated his more experienced ways. As I finished preparing my pallet, the hairs on my arms rose and a shiver ran down my spine as a rustle in the grasses sounded.

"An empress . . ." a haunting voice, as if borne by the mist itself, began from within the fog.

I reached for my sorcery and called the wind to push the haze away, but it simply swirled. The flames flickered, threatening to extinguish our only light, so I released the gust.

The voice continued, ". . . alone in the wild with but a single guard for her protection."

The ghost in the dark fog tsked thrice. The sound echoed.

The fog pushed and retreated as if it had grown tentacles engorged with sound.

"How very odd, these times we live in," the unseen voice finished.

Thalaj brandished his scimitynes, searching for the source. "Mairynne," he hissed. "Grab your belt. Flip the buckle and pull one blade from the leather." When I had the small curved sword in hand and stared at the blade as if it were a serpent, he continued in hushed tones, "Face the honed edge away from your body and hold it in front of your chest. Like this."

My hand shook as I imitated him again.

He lowered his chin and came near enough I could feel his breath upon my cheek—cool as he clearly allowed his own source of power to surface. "Remember what I said? We'll face these things together."

I nodded.

"Now," he commanded, entirely having changed into the able captain of the empress's guard. "Stand with your back to mine. Where I turn, you turn. Keep your shoulders glued to mine and follow my lead as if this were a dance."

I bobbed my head and positioned myself.

"Show yourself!" my guard called into the mist.

A laugh, like funeral bells tolling, rang from within the dark mist, and the voice came again. "I do not wish her injury, half-breed."

My spine stiffened at the same slander I'd heard before from a voice I now also recognized. From deep within the center of my chest, I found my voice and enunciated every beat. "Alto-Trea. Do as Thalaj commands and show yourself."

The Cloud Courtier's face peeked from the mist, shoulders and hands apparent, but the lower half obscured. Though in the dark with a small glow from our campfire, Alto-Trea's visage seemed a replica of every one of the Courtier's caste I recalled from my ascension. As had been the case then, the only identification apparent was an emblem upon the shoulder.

The Swan.

It doubly confirmed the Courtier's identity.

Thalaj turned us so I faced away from Alto-Trea.

I made to move, but a wave of cold wafting from my guard stopped me. He hissed over his shoulder. "Keep tight. Others may be behind us." Then to the courtier, he said, "I would not judge you so reckless, Alto-Trea, to have come deeply into the forest at night. Alone. And for no purpose. You and others have brought a cloud island to this grove in search of something specific. Us, if I must guess. And surely you're not naïve enough to face me alone. Have the others reveal themselves as well."

Alto-Trea's voice remained even as he replied, "You seem parano—"

A shriek rang out in the distance, a sound I was growing to know all too well.

"—oid," the Courtier finished.

No longer heeding Thalaj's instruction to face away, I turned. Something that one might call a smile twitched at the corner of the courtier's perfectly illusion-drawn lips, yet it chilled my blood.

"What was that?" I demanded.

Neither voice nor demeanor changed as the Swan answered, "One day very soon, young Mairynne Evangale, you will learn."

Thalaj stepped in front of me. He stiffened his arms with his blades to either side, readying them as I'd seen him do so many times before he began a sparring match with one of the soldiers he trained. "Why not this night, Alto-Trea? It makes little sense to come to us with no purpose save to say 'one day . . .' "

A flash of blue lightning at the base of each scimityne, quickly lit then extinguished, signaled Thalaj held his magic just beneath his taut posture.

"And precisely why, half-breed, would an illusionist *not* have such an agenda?"

Bristling, I gathered breath to object. But the temperature around me plummeted, stealing my reaction.

Thalaj said, "I have no favor for illusionists. I will see your true form here and now, Cloud Courtier, once your body lies at my feet."

I lay a hand on my guard's arm. He didn't look over, but also didn't pounce into an attack. Violence would gain us no purchase with one of the illusionist caste, the ones who managed the political courts. And the fog was too thick. Alto-Trea remained half obscured, and though there wasn't another soldier in Arashi as fast as Thalaj, I doubted his strike would be fast enough. Lifting my chin, I asked, "*Is* that why you've come, Alto-Trea? It seems a long journey for something so small if you've brought down an island from the skies." I flourished a hand. "As clearly you have by this fog."

Alto-Trea pulled a thumb and middle finger to a point where a beard would be—if the Swan had chosen that as a guise. For reasons I couldn't connect, that simple movement seemed like the placement of another pawn in whatever strategy game this person played.

The Swan pulled back partway into the mist. "Wise, youngling."

I bristled again but held myself in check.

The courtier continued, "But she will no longer hold me in favor if I share aught that would give you advantage. For this night, I shall bid you farewell."

The haze swallowed the Swan then slowly peeled away from the grove. It drifted over the trees and upward still. A silver outline of buildings upon the cloud flashed but disappeared as the cloud rose higher above Nantai.

Pristine silence remained.

Overhead, Selene shone brightly down upon Thalaj and me from a cloudless, starry sky.

TWO

The Witch Wife and the Fates

AFTER THE CLOUD HAD floated away over the Yubar
Forest into the night, I found little rest. I daresay Thalaj
felt as unsettled by the visit as me, because though he lay
upon the pallet he'd spread out, periodic rustling revealed
he flipped from side to side every few moments. The frogs
had resumed their songs, and a night bird hooted in the
dark. As the forest no longer sensed a threat, rest had
seemed necessary. We tried. But after hours of pretending,
I whispered, "Thalaj?"

He issued a low sound somewhere between a groan
and sigh. "Yes, Mairynne?"

I sat upright on my pallet. "If you are as restless as I,
mayhap we should continue."

He was beyond the fire that'd died to mostly ash, and
his form blended with the dark depths of the Yubar. A
pale blue orb, full of cold energy and light, sparked to life
in one palm, revealing him sitting cross-legged rather
than reclining. The highlights cast by his sorcery only
touched parts of his face, hollowing his eyes in a ghostly

visage. But the corners of his lips pulled upward into a reluctant smile. "If we are moving, at least we will make progress." He stood and offered me a hand.

We gathered our few belongings and set out again before dawn. A breeze rustling leaves, animals scurrying, and the babbling river punctuated our hike throughout the day—the only silence nature had to offer. No piercing sounds visited us, and we found no evidence of others within the southern branch of the forest. We silenced our growling stomachs on dried meat as we walked, and later in the day, Thalaj sighted and slaughtered a hare for our evening meal. As we continued until the skies darkened, he carried it at his side. My legs and feet throbbed incessantly by the time twilight arrived and we finally made camp.

The darkness would have been absolute save for the small fire that Thalaj built to cook the hare. Our meal the night before had been light in comparison to the greasy and dark meat of the hare. Afterward, my guard tended the coals and diminished the flames to embers that we could curl up next to and remain warm. Thalaj took first watch, stating that he'd wake me mid-way through the night so he could rest a little before dawn. Though the second night was cooler than the first, I slept better than I had for a single hour in the three nights before we'd departed Arashi or our first night in the woods.

When I opened my eyes, I inhaled sharply and rolled over. I'd expected Thalaj to awaken me long before dawn, but Otarr's light already filtered through the trees. Across the pit with smoking gray ash, Thalaj's form came slowly into focus. He was on his knees facing me. Still on my side, I blinked. His outline clarified, hands behind his back. Tied?

I froze. Beside him, two hulking figures stood, each

with a dagger aimed at his throat. Thalaj's lips pressed tightly together; his eyes were coal black and hard. Nearly imperceptibly, he moved his head from side to side.

A warning. Do not be rash, Mairynne. Remain still. Keep your head about you, his motion said.

Mayhap I should have better heeded the signal, but by instinct, I pushed up onto one side from my pallet and twisted, assessing what danger we faced now. I desperately tried to organize my thoughts with the blood pounding in my ears. My travel pack lay just out of reach. And the scimitynes. I crept my hand toward them, hoping fruitlessly that I could grasp onto one before anyone intercepted my move. I hadn't the skill to wield the blades in my belt, but the thought of something sharp in my hand gave me the illusion of protection.

"Halt!" barked one of the men holding Thalaj at dagger point.

At the start his command gave me, I sprang from the pallet onto my feet, only to find two more assailants. I turned first to the man—burly and bearded with fiery red hairs blanketing his arms. His eyes were the brightest green I'd ever seen . . . the color of the fuzzy grass that grew on north-facing trees. Those eyes flashed with a remorseless willingness to use his brawn without a second thought. I had little hope in a battle with one so strong and ruthless, so I swiveled back to the woman just beyond the rest of my gear.

She smirked, her glance cutting down to my pack. Daring me to try.

I readied my body in a crouch as I'd seen Thalaj do when he prepared to spar. The woman raised a brow. The weapon belt between us taunted. I calculated. Could I reach them before her? Chances were slim, but what other choice did I have?

I dove.

I'd scarcely moved when a muscular forearm yanked me backward into a rock of a man. I kicked and struggled, losing grasp on the notion that we might be okay. I started to consider ways to bargain. "Who are you and what do you want from us?"

"Hush, girl," the man holding me gruffed.

The guards at Thalaj's sides conversed hurriedly in a language I didn't recognize. The woman near my pack responded with a sly smile as she lifted the bag and draped the belt over one shoulder.

I struggled against my captor's arm. "Release me. I demand it. I am—"

"No!" Thalaj snapped. Then, in a soft and deadly dry tone, he added, "*Mairy*, stop struggling."

I looked at him, panting and confused. He'd called me by a shortened version of my name—something he'd never done. Obviously, he didn't want me to share who I was or what we were about. I took deep breaths trying to fight the fear coursing through my body. Measured exhale after inhale, again and again, I willed the tension away, first in my arms, then my legs. And as a reward, the man placed me back onto my feet on the forest floor.

The woman, lithe but stout, fingered the length of one scabbard. "Were these what you're after?"

Saying nothing, I continued to stare at her, glimpsing back toward Thalaj occasionally. When she caught me, she followed my gaze, then released the throng holding one of the blades in place. Drawing the curved short sword from its scabbard, she stepped closer, pointing the curve at my chin. "Your friend there's the smart one, eh?"

I bit down, working hard to hold my silence.

"But," she continued, "then again, if I were a betting woman, I think you're the reason the Frost Fighter's so cooperative. Should we test that theory?" She looked provocatively at Thalaj.

He growled, and I could see the muscles in his neck cording as he prepared to try and free himself.

"Quit playing, Jorani." Another man, smaller and with shaggy shoulder-length hair appeared, traipsing through the camp. Young, much younger than the others if I were to guess by the smoothness of his face and his size. He was almost pretty, except for the angry red mark painted under one eye from nose to cheekbone. He strutted like he owned this group and with a bearing that said he was much older than his appearance would suggest.

And Jorani listened.

"Bind her hands too. Who knows what kind of magic she could call if she has them free. Gather their things. Let's go. They're waiting."

"Wait, who's waiting?" I swiveled my head in search of an answer, but there was none to be found.

Our captors ignored my question.

In truth, I *had* considered using my magic but couldn't think how to use the wind or rain to stave off their attack. The smaller man was right; given time, I might find a way. With my hands bound, it wasn't impossible, but much less likely. I gritted my teeth against the pain in my shoulders as the red-haired man wrenched my arms behind my body.

The brute behind me tied my wrists, and Jorani looked at me with a grin while she poured the water remaining in my skein onto what little remained of the fire. I wanted to object, to stop her, but couldn't free myself to try. Thalaj's captors pulled him to his feet and pushed him through the trees ahead of me. I tried to catch up but Jorani held up my scimityne in front of me, warning me to stay with them. I tensed, at a loss for what to do, but with anger rolling in every muscle as they pushed me along behind the others.

We walked for an hour, maybe more, and my shoulders throbbed. My throat was dry and my stomach roared, but those things I could ignore if I could figure a way out of this situation. The morning lightened further and the trees thinned. When we reached the last tree before the grasslands, the group in front of me halted. Jorani pushed me hard and I stumbled to Thalaj's side.

Cold waves of anger rolled off his body and his nostrils flared as he stood helplessly at my side. The larger man— the one who had ensnared me—came up beside Thalaj on the other side and threw an elbow into his gut. I cried out when he doubled over with a grunt.

Slowly, he regained his strength and stood, panting.

The small man stepped in front of us. He lifted a necklace over his head, and I caught a glimpse of a totem like the one I wore. He placed it in one hand, then clapped his hands straight above his head. With his eyes closed, he pulled his steepled hands to his chest under his chin, chanting something quick but unintelligible.

The emptiness above the sea of yellow grasses shimmered and the air seemed to fold, then wave. My eyes felt dry and began to sting. The vision before me blurred into something unbelievable. I closed my eyes, allowing tears to brew behind my lids and wash away the irritation. When I opened them, blinking against the tears, my eyes painted pictures my brain couldn't begin to believe.

◇◇◇◇◇◇◇

WHEELED CARTS WITH ARCHED canvas roofs, large enough for several people to stand easily within, were scattered about. Dozens of them. As the tsym lifted, smells of the broad pack animals also wafted about. Yaks, they were called if I recollected from my lessons, but I'd never seen one with my own eyes. Their coats were as thick as they were broad. Each wore a harness in bright reds and white, many were attached to the wagons, and the ones that weren't wore brightly colored saddles.

What sane person would ride such a creature? I wondered.

Our abductors' dress had been simple, but the people tarrying about dressed as brightly as the yaks in loose pants that gathered at the ankle. Their bloused tunics shone in shades of red, orange, and pink. A netted belt defined each person's waist, displayed coin in varying quantities, and jingled as they moved—a sound also not heard when they remained under tsym.

The men's hair hung loose, and the women wore their hair covered with a cloth wrap. The vision reminded me of a verse the Hallowgales had forced me to recite during my youth:

Her kyrtel brystow red

With clothes upon her hed

That wey a sowe of led

Wrythen in wonder wyse

After the Sarasyns gyse

With a whym wham

Knyt with a trym tram

Vpon her brayne pan

Lyke a sintian

Capped about

Whan she goeth out

I shook off the words as Thalaj leaned toward me, his voice a strained whisper. "I'm uncertain which rumors of the Tsinti carry truth. Have caution with what you say. Don't tell them more than you must."

Before I'd gained the voice to reply, one of our guards pulled Thalaj away. I cried, "No," but in the next breath, I was also seized and dragged toward one of the canvas-covered wagons. I rounded on the woman who'd captured my arm.

Jorani.

"Let me go. Where are you taking me? Ouch!" I protested while wriggling in an attempt for freedom.

"Shut your trap." She pulled harder on my arm, and I cursed myself that I hadn't trained at all in hand-to-hand battles. Jorani wasn't any larger than me. If I had known how to fight, I might have been able to free myself, but she also still held my weapons confidently in her other hand. Still struggling, I stumbled along.

At a near wagon, she dropped my pack and my weapons but wouldn't release my arm. She climbed the wooden steps and handily pulled me up behind her. The flap closed and the sudden shade obliterated my sight. Hands landed on my arms and pulled at my clothes.

"Wait! What are you doing?" I protested, trying and failing to keep them from removing the tan rough-spun shirt I wore for travel. Flailing, I blinked rapidly wanting to convince my eyes to adjust to the lower light. Three heads wrapped in cloth bobbed around me and worked to get me naked, clucking along the way in a language foreign to my ears.

Jorani clucked back. When my eyes began to adjust, I could see her step to the corner and slather something in her hair just before she wrapped her head in the same cloth as the others. One of the women, a plumper one, knocked me off my feet and onto a cushioned bench to the side. The other two removed my boots, then held my ankles while the plump one pulled my pants and my underclothes to my ankles.

For my entire life, attendants had been present to attend to my dressing, undressing, and even bathing, so the nakedness failed to disconcert me. Their purpose though escaped me. "Why do you wish me unclothed?" I asked, pulling and pushing with my legs and hoping they'd understand the common tongue, maybe that they'd respond. At least Jorani would comprehend. But still, I received no reply. In a singular move, the two holding my ankles stepped back and the first slipped away my lower clothes. I stood quickly, bare save for Tsanseri's cuff and the necklace about my neck. The cold stone burned colder and the hot stone burned hotter, and the woman's eyes narrowed to examine what hung there. I presumed they were Tsinti and they recognized the third pendant—the totem Thalaj had recovered within the Evernight. My hand drifted toward my neck.

The women stepped back and looked at my body unabashedly. One clucked to the other, and the second agreed. With a nod, she stepped forward, grasped the necklace, and gave it a swift tug, pulling it free from my neck. I gulped and reached after the woman, but the other two seized my arms, wrestling the Comtesse's gift free as well.

"Why?" I demanded. "Please," I begged. "Leave me these things." My eyes prickled, tears barely contained.

"It's all I have of my mother and father." If I had to give up the cuff, so be it, but my soul needed those stones against my skin and near my heart.

I relented my struggle; they released my arms and went out the back of the wagon. The plump woman turned. As our eyes met, I thought I read a small bit of concern in her face, but it disappeared as soon as it had appeared. Just before she stepped out of the cart with my necklace in hand, she clucked something to Jorani, who dipped her hands in whatever she'd slathered into her own hair and came to me, goop oozing between her fingers. Having been robbed of the stones, I stood quietly and accepted her ministrations. The smell of the stuff reminded me of my aunt Nadialynne's garden.

"What is that?" I asked, my voice thin and a tear rolling down my cheek. Though I cried quietly, I won the battle against the urge to sob.

"Yak's lard, brewed with wild herbs. The lard protects the hair and the *mynthe* cools your scalp while your head is bound in cloth. If you're going to travel with us, you need to look the part." Her demeanor had become easier, presumably under some instruction from the older women, but perhaps only because I stood there shivering despite the hot and dead air within the wagon.

"Travel with you?" I reached out a hand, wanting to call the wind to cool myself, but Jorani pushed it down.

"Don't, Storm Sorcerer." Some warning danced across her eyes. "You'll do much better if you're agreeable."

"I only intended to call the wind to relieve the stale air."

"It'd be best to not . . . for now."

When Jorani had wrapped my head well and tucked

in the ends of the material, the women returned, each jangling as she entered. They carried clothing that matched their peoples' fashion. One handed a pile to Jorani, who changed into bright yellow pants with an orange top. To finish her ensemble, she strapped a netted belt about her and shook her hips, jingling like the others. They all laughed at fun that I couldn't quite share, but it eased my tension a bit.

The plump one came to me with a bundle and said, "Young one, clothes for you. They call me Detsa. This is my cart, and you'll travel as my guest. Sleep there." She pointed to a similar cushioned bench on the other side of the cart.

I felt a rush of relief as she spoke in the common tongue, but I remained confused as I dressed in vibrant red and pink clothes. My belt had no coin, and I somehow felt as if this symbolized that I rested at the bottom of their society. "You will forgive my lack of understanding."

The plump woman turned to my captor. "Jorani, stand outside." The others left too, and Detsa, now my host, said to me, "You don't need to worry much, but you'll wait here for a bit. We'll be on our way soon." With that, she left me alone.

I sank onto the bench, supposedly my new bed, and dropped my wrapped head into my hands. What had I gotten myself into? What trouble had *we* encountered? It seemed that we hadn't needed the totem after all, so I'd sent Thalaj into harm's way in the Evernight for naught, but that we were now seemingly prisoners of the Tsinti hadn't been part of the plan either. Although, had the wanderers not apprehended us, I now felt certain we would not have been able to see through the tsym. Having watched the little man go through the motions to reveal the Tsinti's caravan, I wouldn't have known gestures or words were necessary. Mayhap how we came to be in the company of the wandering folk would have been our only way in. Disheartened over having lost the items I'd treasured so, I remained there and trembled, wanting for Thalaj.

Of the options remaining before me, what I knew, and what I felt, I decided against Thalaj's counsel to remain silent. A different tack was obviously necessary. We had purpose here, and I needed to do something to make it happen. Then, once I had satisfied that purpose, I needed to retrieve the stones as I believed that bound within them were the very souls of my parents. Through one method or another, before we parted ways with the Tsinti, I must possess those to guide my journey.

The flap rose, emitting a ray of Otarr's golden light, and Jorani stepped inside. She brought my pack and my weapon belt. Dropping the load, she freed a scimityne and twirled it by the handle, her technique deft as she scored naught in the tight space. Jealousy stabbed at seeing her immediate skill with the weapon, the sight reaffirming my need to learn.

"They're putting the tsym back in place, and we'll be on our way," she said.

"Jorani?" I ventured.

"Mmm?" she answered.

Good, mayhap it would be easier than I'd thought. The woman seemed now amicable, pleased to be in my company even. I started, "We came in search of your people."

"Yes. This, we know."

A hint we'd walked into a snare.

I suppressed the urge to spout off the question as to

how exactly she would know such information. Instead, I said, "Then you'll also know that I am Empress of the Nantai people."

"Mmhmm." She lunged and spun the blade, engaging with me but not giving the conversation her full attention.

Blades were her weapon, words mine. I continued, "I'd hoped that your people would recognize that you are also my people and treat us better than this."

Jorani stood straight and tilted her head as she regarded me. "Have we not treated you well?" she asked with the innocence of a youngling.

My brow felt heavy. "I'm not certain I could say that capturing us and separating me from my guard is treating me well."

She looked at me blankly.

I shifted on my bed, uncomfortable still but encouraged that she seemed willing to hold a conversation. "I had hoped that the Tsinti would honor me as their empress too?"

At this, Jorani laughed with a hilarity I couldn't see. She verily howled and guffawed. When she gained control of herself, she put away my scimityne and sat across the wagon, leaning forward with her elbows on her knees. "The wanderers only listen to the word of the Tsinti king, Tamás Hætyr. And even then, his law is limited. We belong to no country. We exist apart from your time, and while our caravans roam the grasslands, we encounter none of your people"—her brows shot toward the headwrap—"unless we so choose."

Lifting my chin, I demanded, "Who is this Tsinti king you speak of? I would like to meet him. Mayhap he will hear my case differently."

Jorani bellowed with more laughter, falling onto her side and grasping herself about the waist. When she had recovered enough to speak, she wiped away a mirthful tear. "A long-passed founder of our people and ways. He travels with the gods alone now, but under his decree, no person among the Tsinti shall be suffered to live within a tennō's realm. We extend that law to a kōgō's realm as well. We will forever live apart."

I had no idea how to respond to her proclamation, but it knotted in my stomach. I wanted to ask what they intended to do with us, to inquire about Thalaj, but I thought it might show weakness. Instead, I simply looked at the woman across the wagon, withholding any expression.

At length, she gave another short laugh and stood.

"Wait," I said, grabbing her arm before she left. When she turned, I asked, "Can I leave the wagon. I need to speak with your witch wife."

Jorani looked at me as if I'd just blasphemed her god. "Soon," she said in a ghostly voice. "She will join you shortly, and as soon as the witch wife reads your fates, you may walk freely among the Tsinti."

◇◇◇◇◇◇◇

INSIDE THE TEPID WAGON, I sat dumbfounded. Waiting. Yes, I could have tried to leave, to find Thalaj, but when I'd lifted the flap to peer outside, Jorani had held a dagger toward me. And though she'd left my weapons inside, I had no skill with the blades, so I awaited the arrival of the witch wife she'd promised. There were no sounds inside the cart, and the canvas muffled the milling around outside. My scalp began to tingle and cool, so I reached up to explore the headwrap by touch.

"Amazing," I mused. I no longer felt the need to call

the wind and cool myself. It appeared the women of the Tsinti had shown me a kindness I hadn't expected.

"What's amazing?" an old woman's voice croaked, and a beam of Otarr's light shone into the cart. The actual woman who stepped inside didn't match the voice. When she turned to me, I saw she had no lines at the corners of her eyes or around her mouth. Her skin appeared taut like a ripe Aomori apple's and her smile glittered. She carried a kettle and two stoneware cups, and a small bag hung from a string about her wrist, her clothing a melding of bright greens and blues and purples. She cleared her throat and said, in a voice as fresh as spring, "They said you'd finally arrived. Tell me why you've come to us, young one."

I bristled at her naming me *young one*, especially given that she appeared my age or younger. The first voice I'd heard from her seemed more in line with one who would address me so, though I had to admit that I truly had no idea what a witch wife was. And so, I asked.

The woman acted as if I hadn't spoken and went to the same table where Jorani had worked. There, she poured steaming water into the two cups and handed one to me with a command, "Drink."

My look must have bespoken my skepticism, because she offered a gentle smile and added, "Don't worry, there is no poison in the cup. I'll drink with you as soon as I have set up here."

Within the warm wagon, almost the last thing I desired was a steaming drink, but I took the cup and held it between my hands. Herbs floated in the water, changing it from clear to a cloudy green color. The woman went back to the flap and pinned it open so that light streamed in. My eyes, having adjusted to the dimness within, stung, and I squinted as they readjusted.

"Drink," she said again, sipping from her own earthenware cup.

I wished for my golem, but I lifted the cup to my lips and took a small sip. My eyes popped open. I'd expected something earthy, but the flavor tasted surprisingly sweet, honeyed mayhap, but the tang didn't carry the mustiness of honey. The taste was woodsier, something I'd never experienced. I took another sip, trying to place it.

The woman pulled a pail from a corner and set it upside down between the cushioned benches, then grabbed a wide board and placed it on the tipped pail. She retrieved her cup, took a seat across the makeshift table, and pulled a stack of cards from the small pouch about her wrist. "You didn't tell me what brings you here," she reminded.

"I'm searching for my father," I said suddenly, my tongue feeling looser than it had before.

"Ah. I see."

"May I have your name?" I asked.

"Apologies. I am called Zofi by those close." Her eyes crinkled, another contrast with the smooth face, as she offered a tight smile.

"Zofi." I tasted her name, short like the given names of the Cloud Courtiers, but surely one of the second caste would not be here. They traveled by cloud, high above Nantai. I peered up to the witch wife. "You didn't answer my question either."

"No, I didn't, did I?" She handed me the stack of cards. "Shuffle these."

I accepted the cards and set my almost empty cup to the side, then shuffled.

She relaxed on the bench across from me with a sigh.

"I am the one you were assigned to await. The witch wife you seek. Lay three cards face up when they are sorted to your satisfaction."

I did as she asked. The first depicted a woman sitting in the center of a radiant yellow sun. Otarr. Upon her head lay a crown of twelve stars, and her feet rested upon the moon. Selene. Her right hand held a sword, and upon her left a dragon with wings spread wide. I glanced up, unsure if I should continue. She nodded, and I flipped the second card. A skeleton stood in an empty field with hands and feet protruding in all directions, the hands each holding a sword. I flipped the third—this one, I recognized. Upon the card, the personification of Otarr poured the essence of life from one urn to another, a sword resting on the floor at Otarr's feet.

When I'd completed the task, Zofi sat forward and studied the cards.

The silence stretched out long enough that I grew uncomfortable and asked, "What do they mean?"

She remained silent for another minute, rubbing her bottom lip. Then, she reclined against a pillow. "Evangale, how much do you know of the Tsinti beliefs?"

"Very little, I must admit." This, I said with a bit of shame that I hadn't come to know more about an entire group of people who lived within my realm even though they claimed to live apart.

"These cards, young one, represent the will of the fates. There are three muses: the soul's muse, the body's muse, but the third muse has no equivalent word within the common tongue. We call it *o drom*, which literally translates to *the road*, but it means so much more to the Tsinti. To our people, *o drom* embodies one's life and very existence. It encompasses everyone you have met and

43

everyone you will ever meet."

"Oh," I said, mesmerized.

"Your first card, The Empress—"

"What?" I slapped my hand on the makeshift table. "Even these cards think I need to be the ruler?" As she regarded me, I felt a touch embarrassed by my outburst. "My apologies," I mumbled.

"You don't believe it so?" she asked with one of the most open and innocent looks.

I shook my head, lips pressed into a firm line. "My purpose is to find Father. To restore him to the throne."

She raised a hand and nodded. "The cards don't usually mean what their names suggest. I can tell you the symbolism, but you must interpret the meaning. It may not immediately seem logical, but if it doesn't now, it will one day. The Empress signifies action." She pointed to the second card. "This card signifies transformation or change. The name of the card is Death, but once again, it doesn't necessarily mean someone will die."

I reached for the stones, a habit I'd developed since I'd donned the necklace after Father's disappearance. They provided comfort and focus, and that I came up empty-handed now made my insides churn.

Zofi went on, "The final card is Temperance. It is the card that symbolizes combining or merging of two things."

Studying the cards and trying to gather the meaning, I couldn't discern any cohesive story. Action, transformation, and joining, the symbols seemed so generic that they could mean anything. I raised my eyes to Zofi, unsure what to say.

"And what I said seems true, the message may mean

little, if anything at all, to you today." She reached for my empty cup, and like the woman who had made the tiny replicas of us, she studied the herbs remaining in the bottom. Coming away apparently satisfied, she added, "However, that they are all of the swords suit means to me and my people that you come to us with pure intentions." She smiled.

My shoulders felt lighter, a pressure lifting with the knowledge that she believed my intentions pure. "But what about Thalaj?" I blurted.

Zofi cleared the tea service, placing the cups beside the kettle on the table in the corner, then tucked away her cards and stowed the improvised table. "Young Mairynne, your journey is only just beginning. There will be many adventures and many lessons for you to learn. For now, let us walk."

I leapt up from the bed, eager to be free from the wagon, to learn more about these people, and most of all, to discover what had happened to Thalaj. Strange how my perspective had shifted and twisted in the few short hours since the wanderers had taken us prisoner. With Zofi's visit, fear had subsided and curiosity shone brightly.

The witch wife talked as we walked, describing commonplace things in the life of the Tsinti—the utility of the yaks, what each wagon carried, and how to identify which wagon was which. A spoon marked the wagon that carried and prepared food, an anvil marked the metalworker, and a cube that appeared to stand out from the canvas marked the home of the reiki healer. We moved around as the caravan lurched slowly into motion.

"Under the tsym, we move slowly enough that walking about is common. Apart from dangers from the rest of the world, we rarely feel the need to hurry. You will remain with the Tsinti for some time before we part." Suddenly, she stopped and pointed.

Turning to where she pointed, I saw Thalaj tending to one of the broad beasts, anger brewing in his stance and shackles around his ankles. I lurched in his direction.

But Zofi grabbed my hand before I could go to him. "Not now. The time is not right." Warning flared in her wise eyes.

I heeded her words and remained at her side even though I twisted back to face the man I longed to free.

"Give it time," she coaxed, releasing my hand. "That one. He will always be there for you. There will come a time when you'll doubt but rest easy as he will always return."

When I spun to ask her meaning, she was gone.

THREE

Tsinti Swordplay

SPUTTERING, I STOOD ALONE even though the colorful Tsinti went about their day all around me. Only a couple even noticed that I had joined their masses. Mayhap it had been a kindness Detsa, Jorani, and the others had done for me, but no one had taken the same measures with my escort, and that seemed out of balance. I watched him for a while before he felt my stare upon him. Tentatively, as if I'd tapped him on the shoulder, he turned and met my gaze. His mouth opened, then closed, and even across the field, I could see a muscle tick in his square jaw. He, too, had been stripped of his weapons. But moreover, someone had also stripped away his tunic and left him to brown in the sun. The dark pants he wore were his, not a colorful variety, and splotches of mud caked around his knees. A bloodied cut showed across his upper shoulder. Worry gathered in my heart. Once again, I'd led him into a battery, and I felt sick that I'd no idea how to relieve him of that pain. I tried to tell him with my eyes I was sorry, but his hardened even more. Thalaj shook his head, which I read as his warning for me not to approach, and he returned to brushing the course hair of a yak.

I stepped forward, once, twice. Despite his warning, I meant to go to him, to find someone around him and ask whomever had him bound what the meaning was. Why hadn't the Tsinti changed his clothes and treated him as the women had with me? I moved, scanning his surroundings, but at the same time, I lost track of my own.

A hard hand grasped me at my elbow and whirled me around. Jorani and I stood nose to nose, and I got a good look into her brown eyes with flecks of gold.

"What?" I demanded. "You've taken away everything that we might fight you with, and we mean neither you nor your people any harm. Why can't I speak to him?"

"Going to him will make his path with the Tsinti harder." Though it hadn't been a day, her voice had eased toward me as she gave an explanation. "Your purity had to be discovered, for him, it's his strength. Tsinti ways are not the ways of the Nantai." She looked down, then added, "He knows this too. Come."

I shot a single look backward. Thalaj nodded, and I went.

Jorani's words rang true time and time again over the next weeks as the Tsinti caravan meandered over the Central Grasslands. Their ways were not like ours. They weren't a planful or ordered people. They gathered each night around a fire with instruments that sang well into the night, rising late in the morning and meandering for several hours when the drink had worn thin. I wasn't aware of our destination, but I traveled along. After I had a chance to thoroughly evaluate my situation, I decided to heed some of Thalaj's old advice. It was before we had gone into Tsanseri's court. He'd said, "Observe and listen." When I'd followed that advice before, it had worked in my favor.

Regardless, I felt alone and deserted and guilty over having left Thalaj to tend the yak and whatever other trials the Tsinti saw fit. One afternoon, I stumbled upon a group huddled around my first guard at the center of a circle. Thalaj had a long staff that they'd given him for his own defense, but members of the caravan, including the ones who'd abducted us in the Yubar, took turns assaulting him with blades. I flinched and gasped, a high noise that pulled his gaze in my direction, but that, I only did once. Owed to my diversion, Thalaj suffered a new blow, sending him to his knees with a heavy groan. Thereafter, I learned to hold my tongue so as to not interrupt his concentration. Instead, I hugged myself as if I could physically hold my anxiety within my own body.

When stubs of his staff littered the ground and the remaining piece only extended by a hand's breadth from his grasp, the Tsinti discarded their weapons and moved in on him with hands and feet. If anyone could take the abuse, it was Thalaj, but it battered my heart to watch. When they parted, he lay on the grass. I started toward him, but was halted again by Jorani. She motioned to two young men from the healer's tent who came and took him to the cart with the painted block appearing to extrude from the canvas. I didn't see him for days after, and when I tried to approach the healer's cart—something I'd learned the Tsinti called the reiki cart—the boys who had carried him inside turned me away.

I asked everyone I met for more information about the witch wife of the Tsinti, but each and every person with whom I inquired blatantly ignored the question. Day by day, my mood sank further and further into a blackness I'd never fathomed. With no idea of what sway the witch wife had upon my journey, no knowledge of where they'd stowed my necklace or my arm brace, and no access to my only confidant, my hope waned.

On a late afternoon, under Otarr's hot gaze, I reached for my storm sorcery and tried to cool the camp, but all that answered my call was a soft and still hot breeze. After the attempt, I felt immediately exhausted and sagged with further disappointment. Even deprived of everything else, I never imagined my magic would also forsake me.

I lost count of the days, but I'd left in spring and the hot season was still upon us. I didn't see Zofi again, which puzzled me considering the relatively small caravan. Sleep came easier in my new bed, and in the days that followed, Detsa shooed me around her home cart in a way that had me in mind of a hen clucking after her chicks. She rarely spoke in the common tongue, and I began to gather bits and pieces of the language. I learned they called the tongue of the travelers *Romani*. I remained lost, but I also began to reluctantly acclimate to the Tsinti way of life. With all other options removed, I decided to throw myself into becoming closer to them. Maybe if they saw me as one of their own rather than an outsider traveling along, they'd be more willing to invite me into conversations or answer my questions.

And so I asked Detsa to teach me to weave and learned eagerly under her foreign instruction with several other young women who practiced the talents required to create the colorful patterns within their harnesses, baskets, rugs, and tapestries. The language became clearer with the continued interaction, reinforced by the back and forth between Detsa and her other students. At times she wouldn't reply to me unless I asked her questions in Romani. On a day when my mother hen had to tend to driving her yak, I grabbed my weapon belt and went to find Jorani.

As I walked through the caravan, I garnered a few strange or wary looks, but no one approached or made to stop me in my path. I found Jorani sparring with the short man who wore the red mark beneath his right eye, the leader of the party that had captured us at the edge of the Yubar Forest. She still wore the wrap around her head but dressed in plain clothing, tighter around her legs, allowing for easier movement and avoidance of slashing blades. When they took a break, I approached.

"Jorani?"

She turned to me, smile widening as she looked at my weapons. Before she'd even made eye contact, she said, "I wondered when you'd gather courage enough to ask."

◇◇◇◇◇◇◇◇

JORANI WELCOMED ME TO the group and introduced Baldeo and Yankos, the former being the larger Tsinti who'd elbowed Thalaj upon our arrival, and the latter the leader with the red mark beneath his eye. "Come, *djecmas*," she said.

The word brought me up short, and when inquiring about its meaning, I added the Romani word for sorcerer to my growing vocabulary. "*Djecmas*," I repeated. "How do you say *storm*?"

"Ha!" Yankos scoffed. "Romani doesn't work that way. *Djecmas* is your people. It's all that's needed." He pointed to the weapon belt I carried. "Now, are you going to pull those things or didn't you want to learn?"

The trio watched me. Yankos leaned upon a hefty sword he'd been using to spar with Jorani, and Baldeo stood with his feet wide and arms folded across his broad chest. Jorani tucked both her daggers back into her belt and quirked a brow. I reached for the hilt of one of the scimitynes and pulled. It wouldn't free, so I tried the other. My face heated when I couldn't figure how to pull either of my own weapons from their scabbards.

A look, one that well excluded me from the silent conversation, passed between the Tsinti scouts, then Baldeo barked a laugh. "I'll get the toys." And with that, he trotted away.

Jorani sighed as if her task would be more daunting than she'd believed. "Put 'em down and come here," she said.

I marched over, eager to learn how to wield my weapon.

When I once again stood nose to nose with her, she asked, "Have you learned to dance?"

Biting the inside of my lip, I shook my head. I'd seen people dance. In truth, dancing seemed a particular talent in some of the castes. The Fire Forgers had stolen the stage at my ascension celebration after the enactment of *Sosano and the Blooming Princess*, and they'd pulled others onto the dance floor well into the night, but it wasn't proper for a lady of my stature. Amidst my people, dancing was an activity for the laboring class of Storm Sorcerers and for many of the castes beneath the Cloud Courtiers. The art entertained lords, ladies, emperors, empresses, princes, and princesses alike, and those who partook seemed to glow with an energy I'd always envied. But the breaks in rank within our culture were customs I didn't feel right sharing in present company.

"All right," she said. "Well, that comes first. Fighting isn't much more than a dance in which you trade moves with your opponent. Except for the fact that you may be aiming to kill your partner in the fighting dance."

Baldeo trotted back with four swords, wooden at both blade and hilt. They appeared too small for his usage, and his reference to *the toys* became clear. Indignation stung in my chest, but I had naught to do but stifle it.

Jorani made a pained face while shaking her head. To Baldeo, she said, "Put those over there for now and come stand here." As she made this command, she snapped her fingers and pointed to the ground before me. "We have to start from the kids' lessons with this one."

The big man groaned, earning a laugh from Yankos that he answered with a sneer and a scowl. Although reluctant, he did as Jorani instructed, grumbling, "I hate the dance part. Don't they dance where she's from?"

I tucked my head, cheeks blazing. "Not really." It was small relief that the burlier man didn't seem to recognize the reasons I'd never learned to dance. Jorani and Yankos both held their thoughts behind impassive masks, so if they gleaned the truth, I didn't know.

Jorani explained the mirroring moves necessary to develop the proper stances. When Baldeo stepped back with his left foot, I was to step forward with my right. When he placed his right foot forward, I was to lunge back onto my left. "But keep your weight centered," she said as she grasped my shoulders and straightened my torso. "Like so, and keep an eye upon his waist."

The lessons went on and on. Side moves followed, then moves at various angles. My first session consisted only of footwork. And by the time Jorani and Baldeo had showed me all the steps, a small crowd had gathered about us. One of the onlookers began a steady beat on a drum. I looked questioningly at Jorani.

She gave a nod. "Now you do it with a rhythm," she said by way of answering my unspoken question.

And so we danced. Jorani and Yankos picked up the wooden swords, and when I misstepped, they scolded, tapping me on the calf, thigh, or shoulder that had strayed from the pattern.

"Enough," Yankos called after a good while, holding out a hand to halt the drummer.

"Thank the fates!" Baldeo said and sloughed away.

"Not so fast," Yankos grabbed his arm with one hand and passed him the toy swords with the other. Then he turned to me. "Now, with someone smaller."

By that time, beads of sweat trickled down my neck and back, yet surprisingly, the herbal balm in my hair did wonders to keep my body cool enough that I could focus on sparring. The correcting blows increased immediately, but soon I understood the purpose of the change in partner, and I started to glean the nuances they'd been hinting at for what seemed hours. If I watched at the hip, he hinted his intended direction before he actually moved.

When the skies grew a dusty gray from the fading light, Jorani called a halt to the activities and flipped her hands toward the assembled people to send them about their business. They clapped and cheered before they left to retrieve their pails, the makeshift chairs they'd use at the night's circle, and their musical instruments. Soon every Tsinti in camp would head to the evening's fire for the nightly festivities.

There I remained, watching them disperse with legs shaking from exhaustion and a grin forming on my face. For the first time in more days than I could count, I felt as if I belonged to something apart from myself. Jorani clapped me on the shoulder. "Nice start." I hadn't heard my name on another's lips since I'd met Zofi on our first day with the Tsinti.

Our, I reminded myself. *Thalaj.* And my lightening heart stopped in midflight.

As the days went on, I wove with the girls in the morning, walked along or rode in Detsa's cart with the caravan at midday, and practiced the dance with the Tsinti scouts in the late afternoon. It became a simple routine, and I saw my body change. Where there had been soft curves before, I felt hardened ridges and the muscles in my legs became roped. But all the while, I rarely crossed paths with the man who'd led me out of Stormskeep, the one I'd trusted as my protector, and when I did, he simply pressed his mouth tighter and turned away. At least I'd seen with my own eyes that he'd healed. I wished—no I longed—to know what labors they wrought upon him, but I heeded his signals and let it be.

There was little indication to my untrained senses in which direction we traveled. One day, it seemed we went north with Otarr to my right in the morning hours, but the next, I would judge we had turned south. The heat persisted. My sorcery that I'd relied upon my entire life to call winds and rains from the skies above remained muted for reasons I couldn't understand. I assumed it had much to do with the tsym, but if I tried to call the rain, the air simply grew thicker, more moist. My new, and hopefully temporary, life seemed pure confusion; the only reliable things I had were working a loom and learning to dance with weapons, so that is what I focused on.

We arrived at the river after many days spent dancing and wood-sparring with Jorani, then Baldeo. The scouts discussed my progress and agreed that I was ready to face their leader, and presumably the more skilled fighter. It would be a final test to allow me to train with real blades. They would judge to see if my clumsiness had left and determine if they felt I had gained enough control to harm neither myself nor my opponent. Yankos and I faced off within the circle of Tsinti, each of us wielding two wooden short swords. The dance began.

Somewhere outside my sight, the drumbeat sounded, and I placed my feet to the rhythm the drummer pounded. Yankos did the same. We crouched and circled. He flipped one toy sword, then the other as we revolved around one another, a lascivious smile growing on his face and stretching the red mark unnaturally. I concentrated on his hip, his shoulder, waiting for him to reverse or begin to attack. He did the same.

"Will you charge, little one?" he taunted.

"I stand taller than you by near a hand, *little* one," I retorted.

"But you are thinner. I outweigh you by a stone."

"I have longer reach." I felt a grin break across my face.

He grinned back, a vicious smile, and I saw within his eyes and a jagged line of his teeth that he'd won battles upon battles to become the scout leader he was. But I breathed, twirled one of my own toy swords, and reversed the dance. We encircled one another in the other direction for many beats. Then, his hip twitched, warning of his attack. He lunged and I parried.

"Good," he praised, then sprang forth with the opposite sword.

I blocked again.

The dance resumed.

"What do you want from this, little one?" Yankos asked.

I drew my brows, failing to understand the relevance of his question, but the answer seemed obvious. "To learn to wield my own weapons," I answered.

"Ah, but there must be something more," he pressed, eyes narrowing.

If there was, I couldn't think of it in the moment. It took all my concentration to place my feet as I'd learned, to watch his tells as I'd been taught, and to plan my next move.

Yankos leapt at me again, a three-blow attack I'd encountered before. I raised my weapons to meet each strike, and after, he retreated on the balls of his feet.

Pleased with my defense, I spat, "Thalaj!" through gritted teeth. "I want my guard freed as I am." I leapt forward, returning the same three blows.

My opponent waved off my swords as if they were feathers and laughed, an insulting and infuriating crow. "Now we're getting somewhere. But there's more still. Tell me," he said, then hissed, "*Little* one."

My muscles coiled and ice-cold rage filled my thoughts over all I'd sacrificed—so much—so many things frozen in my mind's eye. But I inhaled through my nose, pushed the air away through my mouth, and then repeated the calming breath. In the heat of that moment, the time wasn't right to release all my burdens. I pictured a field, clear of all Tsinti. The only people existing in Nantai or beyond were me and my foe. I locked my arms and attacked with singular purpose.

Yankos parried and blocked, sending each jab and hack away from his body. After, he gave a satisfied smile and nod just before we locked into the quick-time dance and traded strike after strike, slash after slash, and stab after stab. There wasn't time for more words; my breath quickened. I spun, stabbing backward, but found myself within his grip, his sword in front of me, poised at the river of my life's blood. Thankfully, his test wasn't complete with that move, else I would have failed and suffered the implied slit of my throat. But he shoved me away, following with strikes like lightning, blow upon thunderous blow, until one landed in my gut and I fell backward, air whooshing from my lungs. Instinctively, I reached for the wind, tried to gather storm clouds, but all the effort did was drain my strength.

I collapsed onto my back. I gasped for breath as Yankos, the small but hardened Tsinti scout, closed in again. Raising his toy sword high and jumping in a move that would strengthen his blow tenfold, he came down upon me. Somehow, I pulled the swords in front of me, rolled, and sent his attack into the dirt.

Time slowed. I coughed and hacked and rounded around the pain in my gut. Thankfully, no further siege came. I heard whimpers, and only later realized they came from my own throat. And as I gained my breath, I heard a splash and felt a splatter upon my face.

I sucked in a gloriously refreshing wave of air, rolled, and stood. The pain beneath my ribs still throbbed but receded slowly. My fingers ached with the tight grip on the swords as I lifted my head and opened my eyes. Beyond a smiling Yankos, a large urn lay emptying water onto the ground; and behind that, Thalaj stood, fists clenched, and pure iced fury reigned within in his eyes.

◇◇◇◇◇◇◇

HIS HAIR HUNG LOOSE from its typical knot, a frame of scraggled waves around his high cheekbones. His skin had burnished in the sun's rays, and while he'd always been lean, it seemed to stretch tighter over his arms. The depth within his almond-shaped eyes sent a chill over me. I'd watched Thalaj train his soldiers for years, and toughened though he was by the Tsinti labors, my first guard was undoubtedly preparing his body to fight.

As I scrambled for my feet, he lunged toward Yankos. The scout nodded to the other scouts, and they moved to seize him just as another Tsinti burst through the circle and clubbed Thalaj across the back. Thalaj coughed but kept moving forward. Jorani and Baldeo grasped his arms just before he reached Yankos.

Furiously fighting against the hands that held him just out of reach, Thalaj kept writhing toward my opponent and growled, "How dare you hit a lady?" Nevermind that he'd so often sparred with the female guard Gaelynne, I was a different matter altogether—his *empress*.

Thalaj lunged again, and Jorani had to brace herself with both legs to hold him in place.

Yankos flipped a wooden sword in the air, catching it by the hilt and looked at his would-be attacker with a raised brow. "Your *lady*, as you will, asked to learn to fight. I am merely obliging her wishes."

Thalaj pulled. This time, Jorani's grip slipped and he swung the free hand toward Yankos.

Yankos ducked and came up laughing, still confident either that Baldeo wouldn't lose the beast he held or that he could easily handle Thalaj.

I wasn't so sure.

"Stop!" I cried.

The crowd circling the scene cheered and heckled. "Let 'im go," one yelled. "Fight, fight, fight," several others chanted. The commotion continued until Yankos held up both hands and walked slowly about the circle looking at the crowd. He finished his revolution standing in front of me once again.

"This *little one* here. She has learned to fight. She

bears the soul of the warrior. Would you deny her such an honor, *soldier?*" He looked at Thalaj, then back at me. "And you, *Empress of all of Nantai,* believe this prisoner should walk freely among the wandering folk?"

I lifted my chin, the pain in my midsection forgotten. "I do." The two words seemed inept as if I were telling a wolf to hold a hare close to his bosom. But they hit stronger than I would have imagined.

Yankos said, "What good do you believe he may do for the Tsinti?"

"If you believe I possess a warrior's soul, test him. All I know about determination, control, and bravery, I have learned through watching this man." I swallowed once I'd freed the words, worried that I'd just sent him into more harm.

The scout leader looked at Thalaj from head to toe, and as he did, Thalaj's nostrils flared in response. Silently, I tried to tell my guard to allow this, that I was okay, and that this was the right—and maybe the only—way.

"Very well," Yankos said at last. "Maladros?"

I'd forgotten about anyone but Yankos and Thalaj, but the man with the club stepped forward, answering to his name. And now that I studied him, I recognized him as one of Yankos's companions when they'd taken us from the edge of the Yubar Forest south of Arashi.

To Maladros, Yankos continued, "You'll have to find yourself a new plaything. Get me his weapons and let us test his worth." He turned to face me, holding his hand, palm up, to Jorani. "I will use yours."

Jorani placed my belt with the scimitynes still sheathed into his waiting hand.

I gathered all my training and poise so that I could

stifle the gasp that gathered in my chest. I'd never seen Thalaj battle another warrior where both used the scimitynes. In fact, it surprised me that Yankos would choose to wield a weapon not his own. Surely he could not have known the movements of the curved blades as intimately as Thalaj. All I'd learned over the recent weeks in combination with having watched Thalaj train for years upon years informed me that the dance with scimitynes wasn't the same as with straight blades. Instead of push, pull, stab, the moves would roll, whirl, and slash. Even a slash with a straight blade differed from slashing with a curved. This knowledge I had in my head, like something read in a book, though I certainly could not have executed the differences between the two with my own body. Though Yankos had praised my growing skill, I remained an amateur, new to the craft.

As two unknown wanderers brought the weapons forward, I stepped to the side, hugging myself to bind the worry within my body and not allow it to distract the battle.

The men circled each other, but there was no playful banter like Yankos offered when sparring with me, and Thalaj had never been one to speak during a match. There wasn't much foreplay in their dance, either, before Thalaj loosed his whirling attack, a combination of a left slash, then a right, the two quick pivots in opposite directions, each with a deadly slash. Yankos met the blows and returned them. The action seemed to roll as blades clanged and sang against one another over and over and over. Soon, they were both bloodied about the torso, but neither seemed to notice. I held my hands over my mouth, attempting to assure my silence. When four curved blades locked between them and they both sneered between the metal at each other, I finally couldn't hold it any longer.

"Enough!" I snapped.

They stopped, and the drums died along with the chanting.

When the silence was complete, I said, "You have no call to kill one another."

Relenting, they released the entangled blades and both faced me, panting. A movement caught my eye and I turned. Zofi stood at my side wearing a wide, satisfied smile.

FOUR

Here Goes the Road

ABOUT HER HEAD, SHE wore a wrap woven of bright gold and fiery red. Zofi raised her chin high toward Otarr in the sky and called to the onlookers, "The leader of Nantai is right. This is done. Wanderers, let us take repast and prepare for the naming this evening. We are to welcome our children into our caravan tonight under the watchful eyes of the fates. Go now and prepare."

Thalaj came to my side unhindered as the exhilaration dissipated and the crowd filtered away, rivulets of blood running down his bare torso.

Zofi took my hand in one of her own and patted it with the other. Peering at my first guard, she said, "Go see the reiki master to tend to those cuts, then to Detsa for some clothing appropriate for the evening's fire." With the offering of a small smile and a nod, she turned and left us there.

Yankos sheathed my scimitynes and handed the belt to me. Then, the scouts went as well, leaving Thalaj and me alone. It seemed he'd proven his strength at long last and now enjoyed the same privileges as me. Though he still held his weapons, I dropped the belt, threw my arms around his neck, and squeezed, heedless of the blood.

He grunted, then sighed and pulled back from the embrace. "Are you truly well, Mairynne?"

I nodded vigorously, afraid to try to speak with how my throat had tightened. His voice sounded rough to my ears, very much a reflection of the wear upon his body and the long hours working under Otarr's light. I took him to the cart marked with the extruding block, refusing to leave him while the healer cleaned and bandaged the cuts. Fortunately, all were mere scratches and, though they had painted his chest and back in crimson blood and might leave scars, they would heal easily enough. Afterward, we went to my home cart, Detsa's, and Thalaj dressed in a burnt-orange tunic and a new pair of green bloused pants with red, orange, and yellow vertical stripes. Detsa placed a bright yellow sash around his waist, and he secured his weapon belt on top of it. The worry upon his brow lifted, if only by a bit, at having that security sitting about his hips once more.

"Do I look thoroughly like one of the wandering folk?" He held out both hands and raised a brow.

I smiled. "Mayhap we both wear the clothes well." My attire seemed more vibrant than his, and for the first time since we'd joined the caravan, the attire seemed a bit more formal, silken skirts embroidered with tiny flowers at the hem. They swished and flourished over the ballooned pants as I moved. My netted wrap still hung free of the coin that the Tsinti wore and jingled as they danced around the fires in the night. The shirt Detsa gave me for the evening was fitted and showed part of my midsection, which I hugged and fidgeted to try and hide when Thalaj set his eyes upon me.

Tended and dressed, Thalaj and I walked to the banks of the river. The reunion had been mostly in silence, but without other details to occupy the space, the air felt thicker between us. Uncertain where to begin, I asked him, "Do you know where we are?"

Simply, he said, "No." Then after space for a few thoughts, he added, "I lost track, but that may have been the point of laboring me so."

"Why wouldn't you allow me to try and help?"

"Think on it, Mairynne. What have you learned about these people?" he asked.

My brows furrowed, his lack of answer frustrating. Observe and listen, he'd instructed me before. I reached for all the things I'd experienced, sifting through them to consider if what I'd learned would answer my question. I talked, working my thoughts aloud. "I've learned to weave with the women, and in doing so, I've picked up a great deal of their language. *Romani,* they call it."

He scoffed. "That is more kindness than the men would spare."

I continued, "Lately, I've had dreams where everyone speaks the Tsinti tongue. It's weird."

"That's a valuable skill, and one that I've never been able to master. Mayhap we will complement each other. You can master the language and leave the fighting to me." He looked at me sideways, accusing.

"What? No!" I snapped. "Why?"

He didn't offer an answer, only a stern look.

I went on, "I've come a long way, and I'm proud of the progress I've made. You said yourself that you'd teach me to use the scimitynes. Outfitting me with the blades was your idea after all."

"Yes, yes. An action I've quickly come to regret." He swept a hand over his hair, now tied back into his preferred knot. "Seeing you on the ground today, curled into a ball was more than I could bear."

"Then you'll have to teach me to fight well." I nudged him with my elbow.

We shared a small laugh at the gesture, then he sighed. "I will. Reluctantly, I will. If for no other reason than to keep you from such a fate again."

Strolling, we eventually ran into Yankos and Bandeo sitting on a jut of grass near the river. Yankos had a fiddle, Baldeo a drum. Yankos picked quietly, and Baldeo answered with taps to the drum's skin. It seemed a conversation through their respective instruments.

"Join us," Baldeo called.

Yankos moved over so the four of us could sit in a circle.

The mood, even between Yankos and Thalaj, remained lighthearted. After a few minutes, Thalaj said, "I wouldn't have made you out to be a fiddle player."

Baldeo answered on behalf of his friend, "Well, his mother named him after the Tsinti who cheated the devil, and she swore she wouldn't have a son named Yankos who couldn't play the fiddle."

I leaned forward. "Who is this Tsinti? Will you tell us about your namesake?" I said, intrigued to learn more of their lore and history.

"Really." Yankos rolled his eyes. "It's not that interesting, and it's a bit of a long story."

"How long do we have before the fire?" I asked.

Baldeo clapped Yankos on the shoulder. "Long enough," he said and began the story.

Yankos played a wandering tune on the fiddle as a quiet backdrop while Baldeo told the story of *The Wanderer and the Devil.*

When Baldeo had completed the story and Yankos struck a final note on his fiddle, I shifted focus to the scout with the angry red mark under his right eye.

He smirked and chuckled. "There you have my story . . . the wanderer Yankos who bested the devil."

I smiled. "So we do. Mayhap you can play the csárdás for us now?" I lifted my netted over-skirt. "Though I have no coin to offer for your performance," I teased.

"It's time!" A young boy came running down the hill calling to the Tsinti scattered along the water's edge. "It's time! The fire's ablaze. It's time!"

◇◇◇◇◇◇◇◇

WE CLIMBED THE HILL, four abreast, toward the smoke rising into the sky. The dancing flames came into view as we neared the top.

Yankos, in a mood lighter than I'd believed he possessed, said to Thalaj, "Now that you've learned the story of my name, that we've battled, and that I've seen your strength, we must call ourselves friends."

From the other side of my first guard, I sensed reluctance in his returned silence.

At the side of the fire, Yankos stopped and held up his arm in an L-shaped gesture I'd seen amidst the other Tsinti men. Thalaj looked at me, but I offered no counsel. The decision to accept the friendship Yankos offered was his, and his alone. I waited with the hope that he would.

When Thalaj lifted his arm in a mirrored form and clasped hands with Yankos, I breathed again, and like Baldeo, Yankos, and Thalaj, a smile grew upon my face. With a few shared chuckles over the battle, it seemed that we'd entered a new understanding with the Tsinti. And I, for one, felt more complete for the connection.

Yankos said, "Now, I must find my wife. We have a little one being named tonight." He nodded to Baldeo, who joined him as they left, the stature of the two men at odds with each other. They stopped at a group gathering with more fiddles and drums, handing over their instruments. Then, before they left the musicians, Yankos swooshed his arm to them as if he were the conductor, and so the music of the night began. It was then, in that moment many moons into my time with the Tsinti and only after having spent weeks sparring with his so-called scouts, that I realized Yankos was the leader of the caravan.

Gaping, I felt Thalaj's eyes upon me, watching me watch them. When I returned his gaze, he said, "You've come to enjoy these people, my kōgō."

Balking at the term I'd hoped had remained in Arashi, I didn't reply immediately. Instead, I considered for several long moments while more men and women, called forth by the music, joined the gathering around the fire. "I suppose I have," I said, and it seemed true that the simple routines and customs of the wandering folk had wormed their way into a corner of my heart. "I don't know when it happened, but it seems you're right."

"Come. Come, come," Detsa interrupted. "You belong to my wagon; you'll sit with me for the ceremony." She shooed us to where she had three makeshift chairs, pails turned upside down, facing the fire, then shoved a plate of cured meats and cheeses into each of our hands.

Across the fire, a woman approached, wearing a heavy patchwork cloak. By the stance, I would have guessed her to be Zofi, but she appeared more advanced in years. A stick in one hand, she lifted her hands and face to the sky, the wide sleeves fell back around her elbows, and the hood fell away. In a clear voice louder than the music, she said, "Tsinti people, we come before the goddesses of fate this eve to welcome our newborns into this world." When she said these words, I no longer wondered. Indeed, Zofi, the witch wife I'd met on my first day in the caravan, led this ceremony. She went to four points around the fire, drawing a circle at each. "With this wand of hazelwood, I draw their life circles. Parents, come place your child within the circle."

Zofi retreated to the side as parents stepped forth. The mother and father who caught my eye were Yankos and his wife. His gaze met mine across the fire, and he grinned. The children looked anywhere from born under the current moon to maybe nine moons past. The parents spread blankets under their naked children and placed a large bowl behind the circle.

The woman returned with a stack of small earthenware plates and positioned three between each babe and the fire. Upon the plates, she placed bread, repeating an offering to each of the fates—the same muses she had named when she'd had me turn the cards. The soul, the mind, and o drom I recalled meant the road.

Meat and cheeses untouched, I sat forward, watching the proceedings before me. One-by-one, Zofi went to the babes and slathered them in something from the large bowls behind their circles. When she'd finished, and only one of the babes had cried, she lifted her hands again and said to the stars in the night sky, "Only one shows the sign of coming sickness. Bring his navel cord." The mother brought forth a jar with a withered snake-like thing inside. Zofi took the jar. "Father, gather coals from the fire," she commanded.

The babe's father did as the witch wife bade, placing the burning coals inside the jar with the wasted thing. The crowd around remained silent as this ritual went forward, so silent that I could hear the sizzle of liquids remaining within the cord. My stomach turned, and I thanked the Triad that I sat far enough away not to smell the burning flesh. Zofi waved it over the babe, speaking in Romani to the fates to banish the child's sickness. I understood most of the speech and felt proud of what I'd learned. When the chanting ceased, Detsa handed Thalaj a vial, then passed one to me. I looked at her with curiosity.

"For anointing the clan's new babes," she said as if I'd asked the most basic of questions.

The fathers gathered the babes and walked the circle greeting each of the Tsinti families and presenting his new son or daughter. The Tsinti each tipped a vial and dabbed something from their index finger onto the child. Yankos reached us first, and he gave a broad smile. "I would like you to meet Janci." He held a baby boy, dripping with fat in a blanket toward us.

I repeated the routine with the vial that the others had done and said, "I hadn't realized you were the leader of this clan."

Yankos shrugged. "We are a community. I speak for my people at parliament every seventh year, but we don't name ourselves leader."

"Yet the Tsinti defer to you."

"They simply show respect. Were I to do deeds unbecoming of a leader, they would choose another. There are no laws binding me to the position. There is no lineage. Had Janci here cried, Zofi would have burned his navel cord above his head also. We exempt no one from our traditions and hold no one above the others. We are one as a people. Wanderers. That is all. Now, you'll excuse me." Yankos smiled and left us then, speaking with other families as he traveled around the circle.

Three more proud fathers introduced their babes to us for anointment, and we graciously smeared droplets of oil upon the brows of Gashparis, Beltrana, and Mizo.

After the ceremony, the music started again and the parents cleaned the pallets where their babes had been offered. As they gathered their things, Zofi came to us with a smoking pipe in hand, still wearing her patchwork coat and a ban of gold atop her head. She sat beside me on Detsa's downturned bucket and nodded toward Yankos. "He makes me proud. He may be rough, but he is strong and just. A good Tsinti leader." She took a puff from the pipe and offered it first to Thalaj.

He politely declined, so Zofi passed the pipe to me. I took a long drag and let it pass my throat too soon, suffering a fit of coughing as the price. My eyes watered, my throat itched and burned with fire. She laughed, retrieved the pipe, and grasped my hand. I recovered as we sat with music in the air, watching the flames and the people dance, and made no conversation. At length, things began to blur and the whirling people seemed to spin around me. They wore the faces of everyone I'd known in my life—Karynne and Yasmynne, my mother and father, the Triad priests, Jessamyne, Nadia, Corwyn, Imrythel, Tsanseri and Alto-Trea, Viordyn turned Cirro-Vior, and many, many more. I blinked hard to try to clear my vision, but soon, the fire and people and Zofi herself were all gone. I stood alone atop the highest tower in Stormskeep. *What devilry is this?* I wondered. A nightmare, certainly, but I felt awake. Lightning gathered in the sky, and when I held out my hands, it struck. After the flash had lit the sky, I spread silvery leather wings from my own back and thunder crashed, shaking the ground and castle beneath me. I closed my eyes, startled at the power, and when I reopened them, I sat on the bucket by the fire between Thalaj and Zofi.

Zofi squeezed my hand just as I started to speak, halting my words.

"Shhh," she said. "The smoke dream is a message for you alone. The message I bring to you tonight is one of parting."

She handed me a wooden box that I hadn't seen in her hand when she'd approached. Without more ado, she stood and left.

◇◇◇◇◇◇◇

AFTER THE FESTIVITIES HAD calmed, I crept into the wagon to sleep for the night. Thalaj remained outside, and I couldn't be certain if he slept there or sat awake beside the dying fire under Selene's watch. But when I emerged from the canvas-covered cart, he was waiting and tending our packs before the journey.

Detsa emerged from the wagon behind me and bade us farewell, wrapping me in a quick hug and turning away without eye contact. She muttered, "Safe and long travels, young one." She grasped onto Thalaj's forearm and added, "Care for her well." Then, she gathered some spun yarn and away she waddled.

Being back in my travel clothes felt bland. The simple brown pants, cream-colored tunic, and browned leather belt and boots were comfortable and would enable us to blend in with other travelers in villages along our way, but I would miss the liveliness of the Tsinti attire. Thalaj helped me into my pack and asked, "Are you ready?"

I nodded. "It seems strange to me that after all this time and after they went to such lengths to keep us apart, they are simply sending us away. Easily and with no restrictions I can see."

We walked through the gathered wagons and around the fire that'd reduced to smoldering ash overnight, meeting Yankos, Baldeo, and Jorani at the edge of the caravan. They slowly walked with us toward the river for a time, until gruff Baldeo broke the silence.

"I'll miss dancing with you, *little one*." His words mimicked Yankos's when we'd sparred, but in them, there was a fondness I wouldn't have expected.

I rested my hand upon his arm, over the downy red hairs and freckles, and stared into his moss-like green eyes for long moments. Whether I'd meet this man again, I had no way to know. And while he'd seemed formidable in the southern reaches of the Yubar Forest, I sensed the loyalty within his soul for the people he claimed as his own. Feeling solidarity with that impression, I could find no words of farewell. So I squeezed his arm with affection, smiled, and lowered my gaze.

When he had gone, I asked the two remaining, "Won't you need to drop the tsym for us to leave?"

Yankos said, "No. Simply walk far enough away, and when you turn back, you'll not see the caravan anymore."

Jorani grasped my shoulders. "I would set out with you on this journey, but Zofi tells me your road will take you across the watery plains. That's no place for a Tsinti. Here." She placed a stoppered vial in my hand.

I looked at her curiously.

She pointed to my head, where my hair remained wrapped in the bans. "Before you meet others, you'll want to wash the fats from your hair and leave it loose. We only wear the bans within the caravan. *Kai zal o drom,* Mairynne." She hugged me fiercely and left us there alone with Yankos.

The three of us made it to the Betsu River's banks before Yankos stopped and prepared to take his leave of us. "Do you have everything?"

"I do." As I said the words, I felt the hard metal cuff embrace my upper arm, sitting just above a bulging muscle that hadn't been so prominent before, and the cold and hot stones along with the totem against my breast. Those were the important things.

"Very well." He grasped my wrist, turning my palm upward. He laid his other hand across mine, transferring something unseen, and folded my fingers. "If you should come back to us, you will need this. You witnessed the movements when I released the tsym before. Do that, and speak the words, '*kai zal o drom.*' "

"Here goes the road," I translated with a small smile—both the words of farewell and the words to release the tsym. I looked at the totem in my palm with new eyes, a long green and black stone with a face carved at one end. When I returned my gaze to Yankos's, tears blurred my vision. "But how will I know where to find you?"

"You've lived among us for long enough that you'll hear a fiddle on the wind. Otherwise, simply call for us once you're upon the plains." He squeezed my hand and released me. To Thalaj, he raised his arm into the L-shape and waited for my guard's acceptance. When Thalaj locked hands with the Tsinti leader, Yankos gave him the words of parting, adding at the end, "Train her well. Don't be overkind. And, after many a roaming year, mayhap we shall meet again."

Thalaj and I followed the river Betsu as Zofi had instructed toward Kōkai, the City by the Sea. Her words echoed back to me on that walk: "Through a small forest, but always to the left, and your path will be true." When Otarr was high, we reached a copse of trees and stopped to eat. I looked back, but instead of a caravan of covered wagons atop a hill, all my eyes would see was an empty field. I reached for the stones around my neck, comforted to have them back. More of Zofi's advice from the night before sang again in my mind:

> You chose rightly when you took leave of your people. Your mother and father walk with you now. Times will come when you'll choose again and again, but one day, you will be ready for that which you most fear. For now, your heart speaks the truth; your father still lives. Though it is uncertain how long he can remain in stasis. You'll travel over the Syrensea to the island nation of Ise, and inland still. Your journey will be long and winding. Face this day's challenges today and leave the rest for the morrow.

As I had slowly come to realize that Yankos was the leader of the Tsinti clan, the clarity of Zofi's role struck me hard there by the fire. "You are the magic woman I needed, yet I met you upon my first day," I'd said, a flat statement rather than a question once she'd spoken her words of wisdom. And now, there by the Betsu, Thalaj and I had begun the journey anew, leaving behind another people who'd found a place in my heart and soul.

Still chewing the last bite of salted meat, Thalaj stood and went to the brook to fill our skeins. He turned, and as he handed me mine, he asked, "Are we ready?" My first guard had renewed purpose now that we had direction, and he walked faithfully at my side, just as Zofi said before.

There beside the Betsu, I thanked the Triad for my time with the Tsinti and for Thalaj. I then turned to him, leaving the caravan behind me with parting sadness but a heart filled with wonder over what was to come. I nodded and said, "Here goes *our* road."

FIVE

Safaia - The Trader's Town

THE BETSU RIVER OUR guide, we traveled south and west at her side. Thalaj caught fish in the small pools and shaved meat from their bones, and I gathered some of the rigid stalks that grew along the riverbed and shaved them clean so that we might use them to spit the meat over a small fire. Seasoned with herbs from a pouch Detsa sent along, it made for fine yet tiresome meals. For the first day, we walked almost ceaselessly; but in the days that followed, we traveled in the mornings, rested during the hot part of the day, and Thalaj worked to teach me the dance with the scimitynes in the evenings. We met no others until we came to a spot where the river cut into a ravine, the rocks on either side rising a dozen feet from where the water flowed. Here, our path also forked. We took the upper trail, climbing over shallow roots toward a small trading village that overlooked the gorge.

"Safaia," Thalaj said as we approached.

"You've been here before?"

"I've passed through. The innkeeper is as sour as an old sow, but the rooms are always clean and comfortable. Maybe we can catch a boat downriver if anyone's coming this far inland for trade. It'd save us a fortnight in walking." He appraised me as he said this, then added with a smirk, "And ease you into living on a boat before we hit the open seas." I'd discussed Zofi's foretelling with Thalaj, and he took several opportunities to tease my anxiety after the matter. I nudged him with a shoulder then, and we both laughed.

Safaia was little more than a cluster of several common buildings, an open area with makeshift tables to all sides, and a large stable. The buildings encircled a pedestal holding an unnaturally blue-black stone the size of a person's head. Presumably the village's namesake, the surface gleamed and appeared smoother than river rock worn down over time. We stopped under the sign reading "Safaia Inn" in burned and uneven script. Thalaj went inside first. As the door opened, it triggered a jingle and another when it closed at our backs.

The room had a couple of windows to let in the daylight and all the accoutrements to welcome the inn's guests—a small desk and chair, a closed ledger on the desktop, an ink bottle and quill beside the ledger, and a door behind the desk. Otherwise, the space was free of either decoration or clutter. The opposing door swung open, no bell to announce the woman who entered— large in both breadth and height, smoking a cob pipe. Considering the effects of Zofi's pipe, I wondered at once about the contents, but this smoke had a sweeter odor than what we'd smoked by the Tsinti fire.

When she looked up, she squinted, pulled her pipe from between yellowed teeth, and said, "Ah, Thalaj Northerngale." She held out a broad hand with knobby knuckles.

Accepting the shake, he asked, "How are you, Sal?"

"Ah, ye know. Taking care of this town keeps me young." She groaned—not very young-like—and sat behind the desk. "Who's ye lady?"

"Mairy," he introduced me by the same shortened version he'd used with the Tsinti scouts. Though, as it had turned out, the Tsinti witch woman had known me from the first moment and likely had been responsible for sending Yankos and his three scouts into the Yubar to locate us.

I shot Thalaj a sideways glance, but only long enough to see him give a single nod and look that suggested I go along. I offered my hand, imitating the way the innkeeper, Sal, had. "Mairy Summergale," I said. If I needed an alternate name, I decided that a last name would complete the image.

Sal stood halfway and shook my hand, then plopped back into her chair with a sigh. "I'm afraid ye've come too late. There've been so many travelers on the road lately that my rooms are all taken hours before supper's bell."

My shoulders sank, but the matter appeared to bother Thalaj very little. "Are there any boats coming up the Betsu in the next day or two?" he asked.

"Not in two, but three," she answered. "I've got a load of supplies being delivered. Expect him just after midday."

As it turned out, Sal also managed passenger bookings for the cargo barges departing Safaia upon the Betsu toward the City by the Sea. We were the first in line for that, so she flipped to the back and scrawled our names in the ledger, using the same rough script as above the inn's door. "For both, the cap'n'll charge ye a copper mon. For tonight, head over to the tavern, grab a bite to eat, and

79

ask around there to see if anyone has a bed nearby for ye to rest. If not, Mac's letting folk sleep in the bar for an iron mon each, if ye're desperate for shelter. Come back tomorrow, and I'll have a room for ye."

In the tavern, Mac handed us a couple mugs of ale and plates of stew. We took an empty table in the back corner, Thalaj sitting in the chair with the best view of all the patrons and the door. I pulled out the small wooden box that Zofi had returned, opened it, and placed a droplet of the stew next to the little replica of myself.

Thalaj chuckled. "It's doubtful a barkeep would poison his patrons, but it's nice to have those back. Who knows where we'll find ourselves in another month's time?" Seeing that my little taster had no problems with the stew, he lifted the wooden spoon and slurped. "It's good. Try it," he said, the words garbled from sucking air. He fanned his mouth to ease the heat, swallowed, and shoved in a second bite.

I waited for mine to cool, then tasted tentatively. The spiced, meaty stew felt wonderful on the tongue after the fish and water vegetables that had sustained us for the last few days, but it didn't wash away the desires I harbored for a bed and bath. Thalaj hurried through his meal and went around the room to ask several of the patrons if they lived nearby or had a room we could let for the night.

My hopes fell again as he returned to our table, shaking his head.

"Every extra room for an hour's walk is full." Thalaj waved a hand at the table. "So, we sleep here, or we can go back to the river and make camp."

With a wistful sigh, I said, "Had you asked me two seasons prior, it never would have crossed my mind to long for sleep in a covered wagon under the cover of a

Tsinti tsym. It'd be nice not to have to worry about a wild animal wandering into our camp or"—I looked around the room at the worn and ratty crowd—"having to deal with whatever night noises will arise from a group like this. Neither of us sleeps well when we have to stand watch against unannounced intruders." A tang of guilt soured the back of my throat over having slept so hard the night Yankos's party arrived.

I hadn't intended my words to seem an accusation, but Thalaj's cheeks flushed with color and he apologized, his fingers tightening on the spoon. "I know I failed you that night in the Yubar. I have vowed my protection to you, but it seems I've already failed you twice. Mayhap I was wrong to have left without a larger party."

Resting a hand over his, I added softly, "The time with the Tsinti turned out fine for me. You're the one who suffered."

He pulled away, his stoic nature settling back into place. "I'd hoped we could both get a full night's rest without a watch too." He shook his head. "Let's go back to the river. Maybe if we trek into the ravine, we'll find a little shelter against the rocks before it's fully dark out."

In the night's sky, the moon goddess, Selene, had waned to a sliver and shed little light. Twilight had already come and gone by the time we paid for our meals and left the tavern.

As we crept back down the hill and into the thin forest, I stopped with a sharp inhale when I heard a twig snap behind me and off to the side. Thalaj spun, freeing one of his scimitynes and scanning the area. I searched too, but nothing around us moved. Several long beats passed before Thalaj satisfied himself that it must have been a small rodent more scared of us than we of him. We moved on. Leaves rustled under foot as we crept down the trail, and the night's song of insects, river creatures, and the lower tones of the nocturnal birds echoed through the trees. It'd been our serenade for several nights, so naught apart from the ordinary that night. We wound down a footpath to the spot where the Betsu cut between rock faces and followed the other fork along the shoreline into the crevice.

At about a hundred paces, Thalaj held up his hand in a fist. "A cave."

In three steps, I caught up to him and peered inside— complete darkness beyond the entrance. Thalaj placed a finger over his mouth in a quieting gesture, drew one of his blades, then opened his hand with the palm up. An orb of soft light formed and cast a bluish glow inside the cave, revealing naught but rock and a small pool to one side. He led and I followed, placing my feet with care on the slippery stone floor.

"It may fill when the river overflows her banks, but I believe we'll be safe here for the night," Thalaj said as he turned back toward me and the cave's entrance, but then . . . his almond-shaped eyes stretched wide just before a clatter echoed within the cramped space.

I jumped.

Slipped.

Thalaj steadied me with a hand at the elbow.

The clamor reminded me of the heavy gates around Stormskeep—the ones we'd opened during my mother's funeral rite of the Giving of the Sands. But the sound behind me had been one of gates closing.

My heart pounding within my chest and crawling toward my throat, I didn't turn immediately; instead I clung to Thalaj and uttered a prayer of safety to the Triad.

My guard closed his eyes and a muscle ticked in his jaw as he, too, apparently realized we'd walked into a trap. I glanced back. Indeed, and seeming impossible, a heavy metal door blocked our exit. When I spun back to Thalaj, my hand over my mouth, the cave extended into darkness well beyond the wall I'd perceived before. Two smaller people, standing no taller than Thalaj's chest height and wearing hats crafted from fox hides, pointed spears at my first guard.

The Small Folk.

I hugged myself around the waist as my stomach twisted. Sucking in breath and holding, I attempted to trap my sorcery inside. What if they'd come to feed upon our magic? *No, Mairynne,* I tried to calm my thoughts. Thalaj had discredited those tales after he'd gone into the Evernight and returned with his intact.

"Easy there," one said, and from the pitch, it was a woman. Or maybe a girl?

"Drop the blade," the other said in a gruffer voice, though still several notes higher than seemed possible.

Thalaj turned slowly, lowering the scimityne he'd drawn to the floor as he moved. The little people danced on the balls of their small booted feet as if they were ready to strike, the girl giggling maniacally. From deeper within the cave, a heavy foot fell clumsily into a puddle with a *thunk, splash.*

"What have we here?" a voice boomed just before an orb, similar to the one Thalaj held, went aglow.

Thalaj squinted, jutting his head a little forward. "Hoaris?" he asked, his recognition and delight obvious.

"Thalaj?! It's about time you made it this way." A few more splashes. The man dressed in furs came weaving and bounding into the sphere of our light, extinguishing his own, and seized Thalaj into his arms.

"Aawww, Hoaris," Thalaj said, disgust dripping from his voice, and pushed away from the man. "When was the last time you bathed? You smell like a drunken dead animal."

The little ones swung their spears, looking between the two men with as much confusion as I felt.

"Come on in, my man," bellowed Hoaris. "Bring your lady. Misha, Kyr, put away your tiny sticks."

Hoaris, with an arm around Thalaj, pulled him deeper into the cave. The two little ones cackled between each other. They seemed to speak in the common tongue, but their words were too fast for me to comprehend. At length, the female one—I wasn't certain if it was Misha or Kyr—said, "Get on," and pointed the small spear after the two men.

I hesitated, but the other said, "You heard her. The tips are poisoned, and we won't hesitate to use them."

"Misha," Hoaris boomed, then slurred his words together, "bring-'er-in, an'-be-nice."

Misha tucked his chin and mumbled. I furrowed my brows—so odd, brooding even, for a boy-sized man. I failed to understand Misha's words, but they clearly showed his frustration. Soon, he tilted his head toward the corridor with a resigned sigh and started walking.

Kyr, at my side, shooed me onward. "Move along, lovely. Move along."

◇◇◇◇◇◇◇

As we burrowed deeper within the cave under Safaia, I had to stretch and speed my step so I wouldn't fall too far behind the longer-legged men. The Small Folk took three steps to my one but had no problem keeping pace, each planting their spears like a walking stick as they moved. They were a curious thing, sized like a youngling but having already reached adulthood. I kept cutting curious glances toward Misha, then Kyr. For all the time my mother had spent with the Small Folk in her attempts to unite the people, I had never had the occasion to meet any one of them. They struck me as peculiar and inexplicably quick in every action. On we walked and the darkness slowly ebbed. A soft amber glow shone on the walls, hinting at more ahead.

Eventually, we reached a wider area, and the light's source became clear. On the outer walls, stones lit from within illuminated a dining area. Aside from the table with four stools, a long counter stretched along a rough stone wall adjacent to a small hearth. Coals glowed beneath a dark iron crock. The smell of roasting meat also enveloped my senses as we entered, but my stomach protested the thought of eating after the hearty stew we'd had at the tavern. Misha went to the hearth, propping his spear against the stone wall, and checked the meat spit over the heat, then stirred the contents of the pot.

Thalaj and Hoaris chatted like old friends, but I was too rapt with the activities of the Small Folk and didn't follow the conversation. Kyr, at some point, stowed her spear and went to the counter and chopped leafy herbs. She made a long chatter, and within it, I thought I made out the words, *"Near done?"* Misha chattered back, then they both moved in a hurried blur.

I blinked repeatedly, willing my vision to keep up. Before I could calculate the rest of their movements, the cooked animal was on a platter in the center of the table with five full bowls awaiting our attention.

Tradition in Nantai held that refusal of offered food portrayed insolence, so I felt grateful when Thalaj spoke up on our behalf.

"You'll forgive us. We had stew at the tavern, and after days of living on light fish and grasses, it's not a good idea to eat more right now," he said.

"Ah, not to worry," Hoaris bellowed and reached across the table, grabbing Thalaj's bowl and dumping it into his own. "I'm half-starved, though," he added in contrast to the size he carried. Mayhap being that large simply required more in the way of sustenance than I could fathom.

The stools were large enough for people our size, but there were only four. Being half my size, Misha and Kyr shared one. I took the last stool and sat uncertainly with the group. Hoaris looked fondly at my bowl until I pushed it toward him. Happily, he scooped it up as well. The confusion on my face and the many questions behind it fighting for my attention must have been quite obvious, because Thalaj gave me a small, reassuring smile and nod that all would be well.

Through a mouthful of the hare's meat, Hoaris said, "You can be at ease here." Then he pulled another bite from the leg and chewed with open mouth.

Thalaj laughed. "I've known Hoaris for as long as I can remember."

"Longer than that, pup," Hoaris barked as he finished off his portion of meat and wiped his hands on his pant legs. He seemed a bit loose with too much ale. The combination left little wonder as to the cause of his smell.

"So, where ya headed?" Hoaris asked, jutting his chin in my direction, a trail of animal fat dripping into his beard.

I bit my lip, wondering what he knew of me.

"It's all right, Mairynne," my guard said. "Hoaris is the one who directed us to find the Tsinti. He knows what we're about." Then Thalaj backhanded his friend and rolled his eyes. "Clean the rabbit from your chin and quit acting like an old sot."

The admonishment seemed more jovial than I often witnessed from my first guard, and I wondered how well acquainted the two had been before. I stifled a small, amused smile as Misha and Kyr chattered, stealing Hoaris's half-witted attention. He stared at them with one eye squinted, and when their conversation died, he turned back to me.

"Evangale," he started, suddenly sober and leaning both elbows onto the table toward me. "We've been waiting for you here under Safaia. Misha says you have the look of your mother, that he remembers Noralynne coming to his home when he was a youngling. He says she showed great kindness to his people." Hoaris chewed loudly, washed down another bite, and slurred, "They, like I, only wanna help."

It struck me that he didn't call me by title, either my ascended title or simply lady. My thoughts went back to Stormskeep briefly, and I wondered if Nadia had ascended to the throne in my stead. Had the gnobles of each caste spread word of her ascension throughout Nantai? Maybe I was no longer kōgō, which in truth offered more relief than concern. But I wondered . . . did that leave me titleless? If so, I didn't know whether to mourn or sing. I wrung my hands in my lap, still unsure how much of my plight to share in present company.

Each person watched me intently.

At length, I decided to offer as little as I could and

remain honest. "We're headed to Kōkai. Thalaj bought us passage on a riverboat three days from now." As Thalaj seemed to trust this man, and I trusted my guard, I concluded that it would be all right to share this simple bit. Yet, for some reason, my stomach still twisted as the words passed my lips. I clutched my hands over it to hide the rumble.

"Are you sure you aren't hungry?" Hoaris said, looking down at the awful sound's source and back to my eyes.

"Quite the opposite," I answered, feeling flushed and queasy as if I were about to revisit the stewed supper I'd eaten before. Taking a deep breath, my stomach settled a bit and I shifted the focus. "Are you a Cloud Courtier?" I asked Hoaris.

He barked a laugh. "Hardly. Do I look so pretty to your eyes?" He wagged his brows suggestively.

I drew mine together, tilting my head. "But the illusion at the entrance . . ."

"Thanks to Misha and Kyr. They bewitched the stones. Same with the glowing rocks." Hoaris waved to the amber all around the room.

My head spun as I looked around, and I began heating from the inside. I swiped at my forehead and tried to refocus.

Hoaris continued, "Not sure if you've heard, but there's something amiss at Stormskeep."

"What?" I asked and inhaled slowly, trying again to calm my churning gut, and blew the air slowly through my mouth.

The burly man took another long gulp of ale, wiped the froth from his beard, and said, "They've closed it up tight. No word about what's happening inside, but there was a great storm over it a moon back."

Suddenly, the heat inside me exploded, sweat broke out all over, and I felt a chill run through my body at the same time. I wanted to know more of what had happened at my home, but my stomach had an entirely different desire. "Is there . . ." I started but sealed my lips, unable to finish. A metallic tang in the back of my mouth started, then flooded. Giving a small headshake and clasping a hand over my mouth, I stood, looking for somewhere away from the kitchen, swayed, and stumbled toward the cave where we'd entered. Before I made it from the room, I fell to my hands and knees and emptied my dinner onto the floor.

My vision blinked in and out, and I heaved again, the rich stew burning as it exploded from my throat until the purging halted long enough for me to gain breath. Vaguely, I heard the Small Folk chattering as I gagged a third time, and when nothing more would come, I lost myself to blackness.

SIX

A Mother's Battle

PRATTLE. SOMEWHERE IN THE darkness, and seeming to come near then fade away again, high-pitched prattle extracted me from sickly sleep. My spine, knees, hips, everything ached, though my back remained chilled. A shiver crept through my body, becoming a full shudder. Amber light glowed against rock walls and ceiling as I peeled open dry eyes and groaned. The weight of a blanket held me down, but the bed beneath was curiously frigid.

When I glimpsed movement and the chattering neared again, I pulled myself upright. The natter hailed from Kyr and Misha who bustled around the cave and tended to traveling packs against the wall. I ran a hand over the bed where I'd slept, the smooth, cool rock at odds with the sticky and warm air within the cavern. When Kyr sighted me upright, she scurried over.

"How do you feel, lovely?" she said, placing a hand on my arm and clearly slowing her speech for my benefit.

Her small fingers tingled against my skin, but she

nodded. Kyr, concern still shining in her eyes, hopped onto the bed at my side and reached for my cheek. I pulled back but then relaxed, concluding I had nothing to fear from her touch if she'd done naught but tend to me while I slept. Her smile reinforced that she only meant well.

Somewhere in my addled mind, I imagined I should respond, but I couldn't yet put together the words. I pushed back the blanket, examining the simple shift I wore.

"You gave us quite the alarm," Kyr said, hopping down. "How's your pot?"

I stared blankly at the small woman, only understanding what she meant after her eyes shifted suggestively down toward my stomach then back as she stood there with hands on her hips.

"Oh, yeah . . ." I ran a hand through my hair, recalling the purging feeling in the cavern kitchen. Looking around then for the room where I'd toppled and retched, I absently added, "I think it's settled. Where are we?"

"We're just in the back cave. The main area is through there." She pointed and moved over to add some more items to the packs.

Misha returned, saying something to Kyr but stopped when he saw me sitting upright. "Good, you're awake," he said at what I judged a normal pace of speaking and passed a small package to Kyr.

"Where is Thalaj?" I asked.

"Above. In Safaia," said Misha. "With Hoaris."

Hoaris. The conversation just before I'd lost control of my stomach came back to me. He'd mentioned something about Stormskeep, that there'd been a great storm, and that they'd sealed the gates. Furrowing my brow, I tried to sort out the cloudy memories, but I couldn't recall if there was more to the tale. Likewise, I wondered about the sickness. Had Thalaj gotten sick as well? It couldn't have been a poison as the tiny version of myself accepted the stew without reaction.

Kyr fished into a pack—mine, I judged by the scimityne weapon belt at its side. "There," she said, satisfied, and brought clothes over to my bed. "They went to talk to Sal about passage on that riverboat."

Absently, I said, "But we have already secured our passage."

I received no answer. Kyr spread my pants out flat on the stone and began folding the garment with meticulous care, and Misha disappeared through the door. Thoughts piling in my mind, I absently ran my hands over the cool bed again. Another curiosity, I thought, looking at the smooth stone.

Seeing me puzzling over that and much, much more, Kyr said, "We spelled the stone to help break your heat. Seems like it worked. The red in your cheeks has faded." She shot me that reassuring smile once again as she finished folding my tunic and placed it in a neat little square on top of the rough-spun breeches. She stood straight with her hands on her hips, then pointed. "Just around that corner there, there's a hot spring pool. Some soap and sponges on the ledge. Get cleaned up."

My eyes popped wide. A spring-fed pool? A warm bath? Not a bucket and sponge beside Detsa's wagon or a cold dip in the Betsu River, but a full pool with warm water in which I could soak away the aches of travel and the stench of vomit? I wanted to hug the small woman, but I couldn't push past my stunned silence.

She grasped my hand to urge me from the bed. I

accepted willingly, relishing such tenderness in her touch. It reminded me of when I'd been a youngling and the way Mother led me patiently toward Selene's sanctuary when I wanted naught more than to kick a ball around with the other younglings in Arashi's streets. I never wanted to go, but now, the memory of how my small hand felt in my mother's offered comfort. Strange how Kyr's little hand comforted me now in the same way.

"Once you're ready, lovely, we'll head up to meet the others in Safaia. We need a few supplies for the road."

"What?" I asked, slowly coming out of the memories and meeting a new realization. The men had gone above to secure passage for Hoaris and the Small Folk. They intended to join us on the journey to find my father. I shook my head. "No. This is something I must do. I can't ask you to come with us or put your lives in danger."

"So says the sick," she squeaked accusingly and raised a brow.

Beneath the thicket of sable-colored hair, Kyr's eyes were wide set, her most prominent feature. Her small challenging expression made her nose and mouth seem more pointed and smaller, but this glimpse darted quickly away as she busied herself again. She retrieved my clothes and placed them in my waiting arms, then made a shooing motion toward the bath. I watched her shuffle across the cavern to the door where she stopped and looked back.

"You speak nonsense, lovely. The plans were all worked out while you slept, so never you worry." She touched her tiny nose with a finger, pointed at me, and left.

Still slow to react, I sucked in air to further object, but she had gone. My aching joints protested with every step, but I could feel the steam from the room beyond. The warm waters called. Blessedly, once I'd settled into the pool, the heat soothed the lingering twinge of pain from travel and the ache of sickness.

When I was cleaned and back in my travel clothes, I moved more freely. The three of us left the cave to hike back to the small trading town. As we climbed the path, I said to both the Small Folk, "I don't understand why you're intent on leaving your home and traveling with us."

"Well," Misha answered, placing his walking stick and stepping carefully over a large stone in the path, "It's not truly our home, just where we've been staying for the time. We owe Hoaris a great deal, so we go where he does."

I pushed a branch out of the way. "But do you know what we're about? For whom we search?"

Misha shrugged.

"It's really not important to us," said Kyr. "We left home with plans to travel. We tried to join the Tsinti and become wanderers in the true form, but even those who live apart wouldn't take in Small Folk."

My heart ached over that, and I speculated how Misha would endure tending the oxen within a Tsinti caravan to prove his strength. I also wondered if this implied shunning had been an issue my mother had sensed as keenly within these folk. Had the desolation laced within those few words in some small way driven her work?

"Where is your home?" I asked at length, failing to understand why they'd want to live apart as the Tsinti did. "And why don't you wish to live with your own people?"

Misha kicked away a small branch, further clearing our path. "Our people have strict traditions, by which we were unable to abide." His words tossed quickly like throwing stars, he scurried ahead, clearly avoiding the impending dive into his history.

Kyr lingered with me. Looking after him and softening her voice, she said, "We were both born in Brennmor. Sons are rare within our people. Couples who produce one can usually produce more, and they automatically become leaders within our people."

I nodded toward Misha, "So he is of royal blood?" These words I said with a kinship that seemed haunting. If as a leader he left his family, we had some shared experience.

"You could say that," she said, a knowing and rueful smile pulling at her mouth. "But he didn't flee any royal duties. His problem was with the ordering. The first son is promised to the protectors until the time he assumes his father's position. The second is pledged to cultivating the fields and raising the animals. The third is sworn to the women's houses as soon as he gains his sexual majority **to** breed. The first and second sons may take a wife at will, but the third may only take a wife after he has fulfilled his commitment. So at fourteen, Misha would have been committed to work as nothing more than a stud for three decades or until he produced a son with one of the women."

Misha returned from scouting ahead and added, "Or if I *had* put a son in a woman's belly, I would have been forced to take her as my wife. Our people would have expected us to *work* to produce more. I'd have been no more than a stud." Bitterness cut through his every word.

I gasped, appalled. "That's—"

"Slavery? Rape?" With a heavy shake of his head, Misha held his walking stick forward, closing his eyes as if he didn't want to hear how horrible I thought the practice. "I don't need sympathy," he snapped, clearly warding off sentiments he'd heard before. "It doesn't matter. When I told Papa that I wouldn't, he said it brought shame on his family. He named me *wanderer.* To the Small Folk, that is anathema. I was no longer his son and was unwelcome in his home. That's been many years, and I am happy to *wander* now with my love here." He opened his arm. "If we have children, it will be of our own choosing."

Kyr went to his side and wrapped herself about him, offering him the support of her touch. As they exchanged a warm look, I felt as if I'd intruded and thought of Thalaj. *He'll be there for you time and time again,* Zofi had said, yet my people considered him ill-worthy of my attention as he'd been born of mixed caste. I cleared my throat and looked away.

Misha, shifting his attention from Kyr, said, "Anyway, the market is in full swing. We should go. Hoaris is surely waiting at Sal's. The man's insufferable around her."

As we walked up the final measure of the path, I began to wonder how the traders in Safaia would accept the small ones, especially if the Tsinti hadn't even welcomed them, so I asked.

Kyr responded, "In small trading villages like this, there's an unwritten tradition. Anyone with goods to bring to market or mon to spend is welcome. There's mixed folk—the casted and the casteless alike. So we're not noticed as much."

"But we didn't bring goods for trade," I said.

"Mon works just as well, and you never know who has that," said Misha with a smirk and jingling a bag at his belt.

We wandered our way through the loose crowd, people milling about a handful of tables with various wares, toward the Safaia Inn. Inside, Hoaris leaned on Sal's desk. Sparks leapt between the two as she smiled sweetly and he responded by moving even closer. Again, I felt like I was intruding on a moment until I felt a hand on my shoulder. Turning, I met Thalaj's worried gaze and gave him a smile. "I'm well. Better," I said.

He nodded, his lips tight.

Misha went over to Hoaris and Sal, distracting the burly man from his flirtations by pushing at his shoulder with the staff. "Do we have a deal?"

"Oh." He stood, straightening his tunic. "Ah, yeah. So, *Mairy*"—clearly, my guard had instructed him well— "there're only two rooms on the barge heading south. You all right bunking up with Thalaj? The littles can sleep in mine."

I flitted a nervous glance toward my first guard, more concerned how he felt about the proposition than any worry I held. But he only shrugged, so I nodded our agreement.

"Right, then, we're all set for tomorrow," Hoaris barked.

"Tomorrow?" I asked.

With a nod, Hoaris said, "Yea—"

"*SHRIEEEEEEK,*" a spine-tingling sound went up outside the inn. Familiar now. Roars, screams, and pattering feet as the crowd scampered about.

Thalaj's hands went to his scimityne hilts, but he didn't free the blades. The inn doors flew open and people flowed inside, panic written on their faces. I grabbed one woman's arm, asking, "What is it?"

"A . . . a . . . d-drr-dragon," she stammered and scrambled further into the room.

Thalaj and I shared a knowing look, one that acknowledged all the implications. This sound was the one we'd heard before at the Falls, while we were at the High Cloud Court, and as we left Stormskeep. A dragon— one of the elder race, Ryū—the creature I'd learned about in my father's stories read from Stormskeep's annals. A dragon, the same beast that Tennō Makenyn had torn from himself, souls ripped apart, brutally leaving the first emperor of our people handicapped and scarred. But if one still lived in Nantai, had it formed another Ryū bond? And if so, who claimed companionship?

"Stay here," Thalaj commanded as he moved through the crowd toward the door.

Silence had fallen outside, and I wanted to know what was happening, see for myself the creature that'd made such a hair-raising noise. My heel twitched, bouncing my leg and through my body with nervous energy, and I disobeyed. Behind my guard, I struggled to get a view of this being we thought banished from Nantai.

Thalaj gained the door and pushed outside. I followed. A noise, *thwap-thwap-thwap*, echoed. Dust swirled. My guard freed his weapons and stood ready to pounce. Arriving at his side, I gazed up. With wings spread wide, the long-bodied beast blocked out Otarr's light and descended upon Safaia. When it came close to the ground, it seemed only slightly larger than the largest of the people scattering about, and the midnight-blue scales gleamed where they caught the rays of the sun. The wind gusting from the flaps lifted my hair. I held my breath, pressing my lips tight, as two clawed feet alighted on the ground next to the large blue stone—the town's namesake at the market center.

◇◇◇◇◇◇◇

FOR A SELECT FEW, curiosity outweighed the terror of seeing a roaring mythical creature descending upon the town. Some held swords or spears in defensive positions against the perceived threat. Some tried to act with bravery and close in. Others backed away slowly, seemingly too enraptured to look elsewhere, or perhaps they worried someone would attack from behind.

But the dragon made no immediate moves to attack.

Sal, a woman who I'd assumed feared very little, spoke with terror vibrating in her voice from the inn's deck behind me, "It's after the stone. Stop him."

The dragon roared, dual rows of sharp teeth and fangs bared in our direction. Heated breath near scalded my face.

Sal gasped, then weaker, she said, "That stone's supposed to protect the town, not attract a danger we thought long dead."

Also behind where Thalaj and I stood, heavy foot falls approached—a prelude to Hoaris's gruff voice. "Sal, go back inside. Try to calm the people." The sound of a sword sang free of its scabbard, and Hoaris stepped heavily to my side opposite Thalaj.

Scimitynes hung in scabbards at my side, but instead of reaching for the blades, I spread my arms wide, swallowed, and called upon the storm. Winds began to collect, adding to the gusts the dragon's wings stirred. The gale I controlled encircled us, the blue dragon, and the stone. All I would need to do is send in more energy and tighten the circle, and a cyclone would rip the creature into the sky. Though there was the risk I'd sweep people upward along with the creature. If I could separate them, I could call the lightning to remove the danger from this town permanently. Thunder rumbled low in the sky as clouds billowed overhead, and an electric charge pulsated in the air as I charged the atmosphere with my sorcery, preparing for the lightning. In my periphery, even the brave people around began to back away from the gathering storm, swiping the hair from their eyes.

I'd pulled the wind across the Betsu and sent moisture upward into the clouds. As the squall built above, raindrops pelted heavily onto the dusty ground. With more energy, I could rain hail down upon the beast, but I held it back for the moment . . . for reasons I didn't understand. I felt a pang in my stomach as it growled, and my body felt weak. Would I have enough strength after sickness?

The dragon lowered its head, intent on me, and I clenched my jaw, dropping my brows.

"Mairynne, stop," Thalaj commanded, no longer pretending with my disguised name. Concern rang in his voice, and he sounded distant as if he struggled to reach me.

I responded, curious why he'd ask me to back away. Easing the ferocity of the storm, I called back the lightning and rain, allowed the winds to move wider and softer toward the edges of town, but I held the rumbling clouds close. With my feet planted in a wide stance, my arms spread, and the power flowing through my fingers, I held the tempest close and ready to strike, but even in the wind, a cold sweat broke out on my forehead and I breathed heavier.

"Mairynne," Thalaj said again, this time with almost a growl.

The dragon snaked its long head toward him.

I pulled the winds closer and yelled, "No!" I tightened my grip on the storm. I wouldn't let this beast hurt him. He'd been through enough after the Evernight and at the hands of the Tsinti, and I wasn't about to put him through more. I ground my teeth, determined to pour every bit of my energy into this if necessary.

The blue beast moved to keep Thalaj in one eye's sight while the other diamond-like iris narrowed to a slit toward me. The one glittering eye implored with me.

Thalaj yelled again, echoed by Hoaris. The blue Ryū before me growled and swished its snake-like tail toward the burly man. With agility I wouldn't have anticipated, Hoaris feinted in one direction, then leapt over the attack. Thalaj tried to move between the dragon and me, but something about the eye contact made me release the storm with one hand and hold it up, turn it on my guard, and halt his advance.

"Wait," I said, panting and staring deep into the crystalline eye. It watered, a turquoise pool forming on the lower lid and leaking onto the dragon's snout. I recalled a legend I'd once heard about how tears from the Ryū held all the emotion a dragon felt when they wept and could drive a person mad with pain, fear, or the joy they held if a person consumed the liquid. But even without tasting them, I felt a heavy loss, pleading, and a vast emptiness. "Stop. It's sad," I tilted my head as I watched. "She . . ." Yes, it was a she, I decided. I knew so. Beyond any possible doubt. With a stronger voice and more conviction, I added, "She wants something. She's missing something. Yearning."

Thunder rolled through the clouds above as they thinned. And though I'd released my power completely, a dark cloud still hung in the distance.

The dragon's gem-like eyes leaked another pearlized

drop, and my fear evaporated. My thoughts of saving the town, of saving Thalaj, seemed inconsequential. She, this dragon, was the victim here, not us. Not this town. I dropped my hands, no longer wanting to speak with sorcery. The remaining clouds, save the one in the east, floated away as my shoulders sagged. Otarr shone, illuminating the dragon's scales as she turned in my direction—a gesture, I knew, of the purest gratitude.

Then, in a single lithe move, she pounced, ripped the blue stone from its mount, and slithered onto the dying winds, toward the lonely cloud in the distance. Her screech as she flew away from the now stoneless trading town chilled my spine far less than it had before. In the place of Safaia's namesake, their protective talisman, a pile of crumpled rocks rested in a mound. And something upon the cloud in the east glinted like a mirror catching the light.

Thalaj put away his weapons and reached for me.

I fell weakly into his arms then, panting. "I need food and more rest." I gladly accepted what strength he offered. After the retching and the expending of all my magic energy, there wasn't much left within to manage walking on my own.

Hoaris sheathed his sword and walked over. "That was something," he bellowed. Overly excited, he went on a bit about seeing something out of legend. Then he turned to me. "You've quite the power there."

I smiled at him weakly, feeling that it took all the remaining power I had to simply remain upon my feet.

Hoaris nodded. To Thalaj, he said, "Take her back. There's some bread on the table and leftover vegetables over the coals." With a gruff whisper, he added, "You should be able to walk straight through the wall illusion.

Just pretend it's not there." He clapped Thalaj on the shoulder as he passed, climbed the steps, and went back into the inn.

◇◇◇◇◇◇◇◇

WITH THE BLUE BEAST gone, most of the traders pretended to go back to their business, surreptitiously cutting glances in my direction as Thalaj supported me back toward the trail to the Betsu. A couple, seeming braver than the others, hesitatingly stepped forward, but Thalaj waved them away. When one particularly large man approached at a quick trot, we slowed, and I felt a rumble in Thalaj's chest as he raised one of his blades.

I placed a hand at his heart and said, "Don't you believe we should answer some of their questions too?"

"They aren't my concern. You are." He pulled me along, ignoring the man.

Holding on, for I hadn't the strength to fight, I walked with him. Although I couldn't let the topic lie. "They are our people, Thalaj." To this, I felt more than saw him release a long sigh.

He lowered his voice, hissing, "Would you stop acting like a ruler, Mairynne? Out here, you must consider yourself first in order to survive. Here, most people don't know that's what you are. If we're going to get through this safely, it's not the wisest thing to announce it to the masses."

Father's words echoed in my ear, *Truth to thine self first.*

What did those words mean in this case where the duty I'd learned as a youngling opposed the purpose I'd chosen?

His caution mingled with my confusion and brought my intent to a halt. "I don't understand your meaning,

Thalaj." I struggled to maintain my breath as we continued onto the path, then downward toward the cave. "Do you believe there are ill feelings toward the royal family? Or toward Storm Sorcerers in general?"

"Mairynne," he said on a plaintive breath. "Let us get you back to the caves so you can rest before we board the riverboat tomorrow."

"I need no coddling," I snapped, but the sentiment held little heat. "True, I am weak, but I'll not have you dismiss my questions."

Thalaj sighed. "It is possible. I merely mean to exercise caution and protect my charge. These people will go about their lives, spreading rumors throughout the trading posts. The next time you hear this story, a bard will likely be singing the tale. We will be away on the morrow, so please, rest for me today."

"On the morrow?" I asked, recalling Hoaris had said as much. And Thalaj echoed it now. Confused once again, I pressed, "Did I lose a whole day to the sickness?"

"Aye, you did."

Another lingering question resurfaced then. "Were you ill too?"

"No." He eased me over a root that blocked the path.

"Then what was the cause?"

Thalaj laughed with little humor. "Hard to know. I'm no healer."

It seemed as if I needed to speak to maintain my upright position. If I stopped, I feared I might fall into slumber at the side of the Betsu. "But clearly it wasn't poison. The figurine didn't show signs, and you ate the same stew."

"No, not poison. It's most likely just a normal twist of the stomach people suffer from time to time. At least your skin is cool to the touch again. Kyr took good care of you." He lifted a corner of his mouth.

"Were you surprised by her ministrations?"

"A bit. Watch your step." He went first over the large boulder that stood in the path into the ravine and held his hand back so that I could steady myself.

We walked the rest of the way in silence, me watching my every step along the rocky path and babbling unimportant observations, Thalaj measuring my balance the entire time. At the mouth of our cave, I glanced downriver to where the water suddenly widened—a curious thing really, that so much water flowed from so little trickling over the rocks. It appeared small in the distance, but upon the shore beyond the ravine, a docked barge awaited, ropes running from the end toward the trees to keep it from floating away.

"Is that the boat we're to take on the morrow?" I asked.

"It is," Thalaj said and ducked into the mouth of the cavern.

The metal doors didn't slam shut again, and it felt strange to pass through what seemed to my eyes to be solid stone. In fact, I had to close my fooled eyes in order to convince my brain to go. But once past the two large spelled rocks that created the illusion, I opened them to the amber light cast throughout the caves by the other bewitched stones.

At the table, Thalaj saw me to my seat, emphasizing that he would get the food, and went to the hearth. In his hands when he returned was a bowl and two large chunks of bread. He handed one to me along with the bowl, then took a large bite of the other.

Spoon in hand, I stirred the hot vegetable soup and leaned forward to let the steam rise to my nose. The smell alone made me feel as if I had enough energy to skip resting, but I knew what the storm's magic extracted from a sorcerer. I'd need the sleep before I would feel fully myself again. I sipped the hot liquid and swallowed cautiously, judging my stomach's reaction. When satisfied that the soup would stay in place, I reached for the bread and asked Thalaj, "Did you learn what's happened at Arashi? Why the Stormskeep gates are sealed?"

He shook his head, swallowed, and said, "We'd have to return to figure that out. Is that what you want?"

Chewing the sour bread, I dropped my spoon and reached for the stones about my neck. Hot and cold both flared in my palm. "No," was all I could utter, but I worried about my sisters, about Nadia and Corwyn. "No," I said, more assuredly. "Whatever may come to the keep, my path is forward. Nadia, Karynne, Yasmynne . . . they'll all have to manage it without me now." I hoped that my decree hadn't caused the unrest, but there was little I could do about it from afar.

Father's words echoed again. Yes, away from Arashi and Stormskeep was my true path—of that I held absolute certainty.

Thalaj watched me work through these concerns in silence, slowly tearing pieces from the bread, chewing, and swallowing rhythmically. If he had thoughts on the matter, he didn't share, and when I held my silence, he put down the crust and said, "All right. Now, can you tell me what happened back there in Safaia with that dragon?"

I shook my head. "I wish I could, but I haven't a clue."

He pursed his lips and ran a thumb over the table's rough wood. "Well and so. Why did you call the storm?"

Dropping my eyes to my soup, I murmured, "It's what I could do to protect you." Though the words spoke only of fact, I expected his ire.

He didn't disappoint, his fist crumpling the crust just before it sailed into the coals. He stood and paced the kitchen. "I can protect myself, Mairynne. But I cannot protect you from harm you'd bring upon yourself." His voice was deeper than normal and, if it wasn't loud, it sounded hard like the walls of the cavern in which we sat. A chill filled the cavern, his sorcery flaring cold with his temper.

In the rational part of my mind, I never questioned his ability to protect himself, but I'd already put him through so much. It sickened me that he hadn't been able to prevent the beating he'd taken when he'd gone upon my errand in the Evernight. For all his prowess, he wasn't invincible. Patiently, I dipped the bread into the soup and took another bite, watching him. I'd let his anger run out before speaking again. After several trips back and forth before the hearth, he sat.

He searched my face and said, "Protecting *you* is why I am here. Yet I am helpless if you overuse your own magic until . . ." He groaned, sliding a hand through his dark hair. "Could you consider being a bit less willful?"

Willful. I frowned. The word my mother and Mother Feathergale had used for me as a youngling.

I finished the soup, and some energy flowed through me again, or at least my thoughts seemed to clear. Thalaj remained quiet, and the silence grew uncomfortable. The echo of Thalaj's phrasing opened a wound, scrubbed it around in the dirt, and made it as raw as it had ever been.

My gaze met his, then darted away again, but finally I relented. "I'll try." I answered with little confidence. "That is as much as I can promise."

He nodded, seeming to accept this little bit.

I went to stand but hesitated. Though I felt better, I still needed the rest to return my strength before tomorrow, but I had one other bit of curiosity rumbling around in my mind. "Thalaj?"

"Yes?"

"What do you know of dragon lore?"

SEVEN

The City by the Sea

OUR CABIN ON THE barge was so small that Thalaj and I could barely walk around one another, and if we put our packs on the floor, we couldn't open the door. We decided to stow them on the bunk until it was time to sleep, and how we'd position ourselves for sleep in the tiny space remained a question. We'd just turned to go above deck when the barge lurched away from the shoreline and I stumbled.

Thalaj reached out to stabilize me, finding some unfathomable mirth in my loss of balance. "Did I not warn you that you being on a ship would make you feel different all over? You'll grow accustomed to the movement."

"And when have you had time to gain your legs at sea?"

He smirked and waggled a brow. "No time recently, but my training with weapons keeps my balance tuned better than most."

Before we left our packs, I tucked my coin purse out of

sight. Thalaj did the same. Hoaris and the Small Folk had traded well at the market yesterday, and we divided the proceeds of both mon and goods by weight according to what we could each carry. Before leaving Stormskeep, I'd never dealt with irons, coppers, bronze pieces, or the mon strings I'd seen upon the traders' belts within the trading town. All I had ever needed was to instruct the council or the priests, and everything coin could buy would appear without need for my consideration. It felt passing strange to be carrying around the heavy pouch of mon coins.

Outside the berth, we took care to pull the door tight so it didn't swing when unattended. With the latches well worn, it took some thought to avoid having it hit someone walking down the skinny hall. We climbed four rickety steps, pushing the hatch open above and emerging onto the deck.

When that morning had arrived, I'd slept well and was up before the others within the cavern. My energy had persisted even after we boarded the small trading barge. As we emerged in the blazing sun above, the fresh air lightened my step even more. Captain Jerek barked orders to the four men rowing the boat away from the shore and moved about collecting the ropes that had tied off the barge to the trees. He stopped when he sighted us and came over wearing a half-cocked smile and clearly chewing on something in the side of his mouth.

"How long will we have to sail until we reach the City by the Sea," I asked.

Jerek looked up to the sky; birds flew downriver overhead. "Two nights journey to Kōkai," he said, tossing a coiled rope into a bin and standing tall with hands on his hips. Sizing me up, he said, "Unless you want to call the wind to push us along a little faster."

The suggestion stirred temptation.

However, I hadn't a chance to answer when Thalaj stepped from behind and wedged himself between me and Captain Jerek. I rested a hand on his arm, silently asking him not to try to protect me in this situation. The captain may have been ignorant to the fact that I'd exhausted my storm magic in Safaia's square the day before, and his request seemed only to serve the interest of time.

Jerek read Thalaj's manner too and held up his hands as if to surrender. "No ill intent, but you put on quite the show yesterday with that dragon. A bit of the storm's magic, eh? Too bad you let it go. The scales would've fetched a high price in the city downriver."

Heat suffused my face as I learned how wrong I'd been. A blend of chagrin and relief boiled within—a confused tangle. I'd sympathized with the sad blue dragon despite all the lore told me they were dangerous, the enemy. Then there was guilt over whatever I'd deprived the traders of; but intermingled with that truth, I felt a weird, angry sensation, mayhap offended that he reduced such a magnificent creature to only the value of mon her scales would bring. Did they not realize she felt things as keenly as we did? Could they not see that in her eyes? Why did people seem to only consider what would line their pockets? Yet, of course, I'd never been concerned with prices of things before. A symptom of living in the keep, of being raised a royal, of never wanting for anything, mayhap. I couldn't know, but it seemed that this sailor and trader only cared to make his way in the world.

The notion added substance to my being and the duty I might one day hold as true ruler of the Nantai people. I couldn't argue with his basic need to earn his living. Only deep inside, there burned a desire that begged to crawl up my throat and lash out at him. Whatever his motives, slaying a dragon for its scales and the mon he'd make was not honorable, not when she was only trying to protect her unhatched youngling.

I turned away before I said something that might anger the captain of the ship and lose us the ride down the Betsu. Swallowing, I gathered my wits and said over my shoulder to Jerek, "I cannot explain how I know, but the blue dragon meant no harm to the people of Safaia."

"Well, little lady, I'm not so sure about that. According to all the bard's tales, they have a white-hot hatred for the Nantai people. It was more likely the lightning you called that scared her away." Jerek leaned over and spat off the side of the barge. "Anyway, you're welcome on most parts of the boat. Stay out of the rowing pits though."

Hoaris, Misha, and Kyr surfaced from below just as he returned to work.

Jerek gave Hoaris a distasteful glare. "And keep those Small Folk out of sight when we pass through towns or by other ships." He chewed on whatever he held in his mouth, then added, "And out from under my feet."

I startled at the slight and opened my mouth to retort when the boat's nose distracted me, pointing toward the other shore. Absently, and to no one in particular, I asked, "Don't we need to go that way?" I gestured. "Downriver."

The captain pivoted back around to me, grabbed my arm, and pointed to the middle of the river. "See that dark patch there? With the ripples."

I nodded. It looked black against the rest of the dark-green-tinged river.

"That's where we're headed. Water's deep there and flows the fastest." On that abrupt note, he left us.

Hoaris and Thalaj both chuckled at my astonished look while Misha and Kyr cackled to one another. We went to the railing, and I looked down into greenish water, shocked that I could still see the stones on the riverbed. "Should make for an interesting ride," I mused to Thalaj.

The next days followed quietly. Hoaris played dice with some of the crew, earned a few irons and coppers here and there, and taught me the game in the dark hours under an orb of light within the darkness.

The first night, when it came time to sleep and Hoaris and the little people had retired to their cabin, Thalaj and I faced off awkwardly within our small space. Even though we'd been traveling alone together for some time, something hummed in the air between us. We met toe-to-toe, arms fidgeting and neither of us knowing where to turn or stand to relieve the strange charge. I giggled like I hadn't since I was a young girl, and eventually, I stilled within the dark and silence, allowing my eyes to adjust. I wanted him to touch me, but Thalaj simply smiled, reached around me, and grabbed the pack from the bed. He curled up on the floor in front of the door, using the pack as his pillow, and pulled a rough blanket under his chin. With a longing sigh, I crawled into the bunk and went to sleep.

The next night, the routine seemed easier, and on the second morning, we awoke to bustling, clanking, and shouting above deck. I turned to the cabin wall so that Thalaj could dress, then he stepped outside to give me privacy to do the same. Clothed, I went above deck and saw stretched before the small barge a sprawling white stone city, green veins running through the marbled rocks used to construct the walls and buildings rising up from the river. The mouth of the Betsu yawned into the Syrensea before us. Flags flew from the towers along the wall, and a towering keep overlooked the city. From the river, Kōkai glistened under Otarr's gaze, and I wondered how its white stones would appear under Selene's silvery glow. Mayhap we'd remain long enough to see that sight or sail away at night upon one of the large ships with the many-colored sails along the dock in the far distance.

Since the incident Aunt Nadia had explained, when Karynne had been held captive by the Small Folk King, Father had restricted us from traveling. There and then on the deck of that small and creaking barge, my chest burned with desire to see this city. I felt a passion for the newness of this sight—one I hadn't known existed within—and I reached again for the stones at my neck. They didn't flare this time in my grasp, so this city likely held little to do with my path. But something entirely different within me screamed to explore all the streets here, to meet the people, and to see and do and experience all this city had to offer, as well as much, much more. On a sharp inhale, I scolded myself for the frivolity. Purpose had driven me here, and seasons had already passed while we roamed under the Tsinti tsym. This was but the beginning of my real journey, and I had duties to uphold . . . to find my father and restore Tennō Atheryn Evangale to his rightful place on the Serpentine Throne. On that reflection, the stone heated against my palm, reinforcing the rightness of my mission.

Decided. Once I had fulfilled my duty, and only then, would I return to discover more of this new curiosity brewing within my heart.

◇◇◇◇◇◇◇

JEREK AND HIS FOUR oarsmen bustled about the deck above; the captain's muffled orders sharply different from how they'd been in the days before. Below, while I dressed, the footsteps beat out a chaotic rhythm on the deck boards. Thalaj had me braid my hair before I went above deck, commenting how we were fortunate the treasures hadn't yet minted my first year's mons or distributed them into the world before we left on this journey. As such, Hoaris and Thalaj claimed reasonable confidence that the average person wouldn't recognize me, and in truth, they worried more about the renowned emperor's guard who wielded curved double blades in each hand. For that, Thalaj stowed his scimitynes and only visibly carried a set of straight daggers strapped to either hip. Standing between Hoaris and Thalaj, I marveled as the green-veined walls grew by small measures over the course of our approach.

When the barge felt somewhat stable against the smaller docks still inside the mouth of the Betsu and some ways from the larger ships and bustling port into the city, the crew helped us step onto a set of planks. Underfoot, they seemed only a bit more stable than the barge's deck. The Small Folk hopped over the gap, each with a two-footed leap, and I had to stretch to make the expanse safely. Hoaris held my hand, helping me across as Thalaj moved over to where Jerek tied off the boat.

The captain stood and accepted a small pouch with the mons that served as the final payment for our passage.

As he handed it over, Thalaj asked, "Any idea which of the long ships we might gain passage upon?"

Jerek spat into the water, a repulsive action to which I averted my eyes toward the water below the pier. Between the river's calm waters and the wavy sea seemed to be a collecting spot for leaves, sticks, some discarded papers, and other debris. Jerek's brown foamy phlegm drifted into the refuse, and I lifted a lip in disgust. I had little fondness for the man who commanded the barge, but he'd navigated a true and timely course to the City by the Sea. After all, we'd arrived even ahead of his projection.

The captain wiped his mouth in the elbow of his already browned sleeve—clearly not the first time he'd done so—and asked in turn, "Where are you headed?"

"Across the Syrensea, to Ise," Thalaj answered on our behalf.

Jerek tucked the tail of his shirt into his breeches, considering with the motion. "You might have some trouble with that, but if anyone will provide that passage, they'll be over there." He pointed to the long dock teeming with larger ships.

The five of us gazed in the direction he pointed and listened intently to his continued instruction. "You'll see the flags that tell where each ship is destined. Blue means they're going north, toward the Iced Plains. There'll probably be a few of those this time of year making the last voyage before the ice gets too thick to pass." Jerek chewed a bit, then went on, "Yellow means south, along the Copper Coast. Green, they're heading to Lu Galen on the Vesterisles. But you might have the best luck if you can find someone flying a white flag."

Hoaris folded his arms over his chest and grunted for Jerek to continue.

"Those are the ships for hire. They go where they can for the money, but finding one to cross the Syrensea . . . well, that'll be quite the feat." Jerek wove between us and went back to securing his boat. When done, he grabbed a pack, tossed in the purse, and slung it over his shoulder. "Thank ya much for th' fare. Take care now." He tipped his head in the direction of the city, and his men joined him.

My party, increased by three after our time at Safaia, stood there on the dock watching them find footing atop the shifting pebbles as they ambled away. When they were nearly out of voice's reach, the captain turned back and shouted with hand cupped at his mouth, "And you might want to hide the Small Folk while you're askin' around."

We walked to the shore. Even after only two days aboard the riverboat, it felt odd to be on solid ground once again, the rocks slipping from under my boot soles as we strode toward the long dock.

Several steps led upward to the pier, and waves crashed around the stones beneath supporting the weight. One plankway jutted into the city and the other led to the large boats docked out beyond where the waves crashed into the shore. I went for the wooden steps but stopped when I realized Misha and Kyr hadn't followed. Rather, they'd pulled Hoaris to the side.

Misha placed a couple of clear stones in his hand. "Shake these together when we're ready to leave the city. We won't be of any help to you up there. More harm likely."

"Same for within the city," Kyr jumped in.

I called down, "Where will you go?"

Kyr grinned up at me, shielding the light of Otarr from her eyes with a raised hand. "Never you worry, lovely. We have the ways of the Small Folk, so we'll be around."

Hoaris put the stones in his pocket and shook Misha's child-sized hand. When the burly man came to join Thalaj and me at the stairs, I climbed. I peered back to find the little ones were nowhere in sight. Hoaris clapped a hand on my shoulder with a chuckle. "Like she said, *Never you worry, lovely.* Come along this way; they'll be fine."

The imitation of Kyr from his bearded mouth was passing strange, and as I'd grown closer to him over the dice games, I backhanded his arm lightly to scold him for poking fun. We shared a laugh, but humor faded as we turned toward the task at hand.

Passage across the Syrensea.

Thalaj stopped and faced us. "Let's take a look at all along the way, then we can decide which ones to approach." His voice seemed wary but, as was his usual demeanor, he set his mind wholly to the chore.

Sighting only a couple of white flags, I feared our chances for success were slim.

Jerek had predicted accurately; the majority of the ships flew yellow flags, signaling their southward destinations, but a couple would sail north for the Iced Plains or west to the Vesterisles and the city Lu Galen. I counted only three flying white flags by the time we'd reached the far end of the docks.

Thalaj crossed his arms over his chest. "It may be best if we learn the cost for trips north and south before approaching one of the for-hire ships."

Hoaris gave an agreeing nod. "It'll be a good baseline to begin our bargaining."

Again, being the least experienced with such matters, I couldn't follow their logic. I moved closer. "We do not know how far the journey across the Syrensea is. How do we compare such things?"

Thalaj remained silent, scanning the representatives standing on the docks, but Hoaris made a throaty sound and answered, "We don't know anything. The best we can do is guess and see if someone will take the offer. There's little reason to trading and bartering as it mostly hinges on what one person finds valuable."

My first guard tilted his head toward a ship heading north. "I'll speak with him. The two of you go to the yellow flag there." He nodded to the other side of the dock.

I stood beside Hoaris in silence as he opened the

conversation. "How are the seas?" he asked looking over the waters to the west.

"They can start getting rough this time of year, but not so much to the south. Are you destined for the Copper Coast?" He looked past us to where Thalaj spoke with another, a ship flying a blue flag.

Hoaris shifted to block his view. "We're looking to leave the city but have no set destination in mind. How many can you carry on your ship there?"

The man looked to the sky, seeming to calculate. "We have room for seven more. It'll be a copper plus two iron mon each if you're heading our way."

Without any point of reference for if the pricing was just, I held my tongue and willed my expression serene.

Hoaris pursed his lips and stroked a hand over his beard. "Seems fair. I'll talk with my mate over there and get back to you. Many thanks."

The man called after as we turned, "You'd best hurry with deciding. We'll be full up before the morn."

Returning to Thalaj, we shared the cost of each option among the three of us. Those amounts in mind, we approached the closest ship flying a white flag. A grungy man stepped forward. His hair appeared not to have seen a comb in years, and he made Jerek's habit of chewing and spitting seem clean, but the boat behind him looked pristine.

Thalaj nodded toward the long black hull. "She's pretty."

"Aye, she's a beaut," answered the scroungy man.

They didn't exchange names, but Thalaj went straight to talking business. I assumed that if we struck a deal, we'd learn his name then. Hoaris and I hung back while the business ensued, but stood close enough to hear the exchange.

"You're her captain?" Thalaj asked.

The man cocked his head sideways with a squint. "That I am."

"What's your charge?"

" 'At'll depend on where ye're headed."

"Where do you sail?"

"Been all over. Where's your fancy?"

I liked the man less and less with every word, every question he answered with his own question. He moved closer to Thalaj, seemingly emphasizing a more shady intent. His voice to me slithered like a snake as he darted his tongue between his lips at each pause. Thalaj moved into a wider stance with one foot forward, a position I'd grown familiar with after training with both him and Yankos's Tsinti scouts. He could pounce and slit this man across the throat before anyone could blink, yet I recognized it not as an aggressive move, but as a defense against whatever danger he sensed.

"We're looking to travel beyond the Vesterisles." My first guard kept the description vague, reinforcing an uncertainty I had growing in the pit of my stomach about this dealing.

The man rubbed his stubbled chin. "Into the Syrensea?"

Thalaj nodded.

"Whaddye offerin'?" With everything he said, his tongue seemed to slip more into a crusty and clipped kind of speech.

"Well," started Thalaj, "it seems that those sailing

north are charging a bronze mon per head." He turned toward us. "What did you say they were charging to go south?"

"Half that to the Copper Coast," Hoaris answered.

Thalaj folded his arms and turned back to the man. "I'm thinking we'd be somewhere in between."

I held utterly still, surprised by the low value of the offer and knowing that the journey across the Syrensea would extend well beyond the known destinations along the Nantai coast. The grungy man busted out in hoarse laughter, spittle flying from his lips. He blubbered on for several long minutes, slapping his leg and wiping tears, whether real or pretended, from under his eyes. "Have ye any idea what it takes to sail into the Syrensea?"

Thalaj, I knew, did not possess this insight. But he held his ground and kept silent as if expecting that the man would assume he understood.

"I'd risk me ship and every soul aboard. Not many a ship return from that venture." The man walked back to his stool, bow-legged, sat down, and pulled out a knife with which he proceeded to clean the grime from under a thumbnail. I fought the urge to raise a lip in disgust.

"Ye see," he said distantly, "ye have two problems."

"And what are those?" Thalaj remained utterly still, cool waves wafting from him.

"First, I had to let me crew go on account of no business. So ye'd have to staff me boat here."

I had no idea what the pay for a sailor was, but it couldn't have been within the reach of the coin we had in our small purses.

Stoic as ever, Thalaj simply said, "And the second?"

"Ye'll have to stock the ship for the trip." He looked up, flicking a chunk into the sea. "For the whole crew, there and back."

I couldn't hold back any longer. "That's robbery. Certainly you'd profit from the travels in other ways. We'd do better to buy your ship directly."

"I'll not be sellin'." The grubby man crossed his legs, making himself more comfortable. "If ye can't agree to my price, check the others then. I'll match any price ye find."

Thalaj raised a brow at the promise. "Well, sir, we thank you for your time, and mayhap we'll return with an offer." He turned away, then looked over his shoulder, "That is if we feel you'll have reason and consider it."

He called after us, but Thalaj whispered to me, "Don't look back. Let him wonder."

Several paces away, we stopped to further discuss.

"We surely don't have that kind of mon." I whispered, not truly comprehending what it'd cost to fully stock a ship. "How are we supposed to gain passage if they're going to ask us to foot the entire cost."

Hoaris guffawed. "She's new to this travel thing, eh?"

"Mairynne," Thalaj said, "They always start high, which is the reason I started so low. We need more room to negotiate. Let's talk to the others."

The second white-flagged boat had its own crew, and I liked the nature of the woman who stood at the plank bargaining for passengers. She bantered just as confidently as the men who lined the docks, and she worked the crowd even better with an ample amount of cleavage showing. "Come aboard the *Seaduction*," she hawked. "Your destination can be ours too."

When we approached her asking about sailing into the Syrensea, she shook her head vigorously and shooed us away, claiming the journey too unpredictable. After the second miss, we went to the third. I looked back over my shoulder to the grungy man who watched us surreptitiously as we went, still imagining him every bit the serpent lying in wait. And despite the fear we may remain without transport, I resolved not to travel with the scoundrel.

At the third boat, a man stood beside a table under a white flag. Far less boisterous than the woman working the crowd at the *Seaduction*, he tinkered with a gadget. A shipwright, perhaps. In comparison to the man at the first ship, he presented a cleaner appearance, save for the grease around his fingernails. He seemed reasonable and offered a shy smile as they approached. But he had to take the request on board to ask the captain before he could make an offer. Unfortunately, his offer was roughly the same as the slimy sailor's.

After exhausting the options, Thalaj stood for a long moment looking at people milling about the dock, the other passenger long ships, and the fishing boats on an adjacent dock before he spoke again. "We should venture into the city. Maybe we'll get a better idea of our possibilities there. At least we can inquire about sailors for hire and what it'd cost to stock a ship."

Seeming like our best option, we ambled across the plank, following a long line of people in one direction while passing fisherpeople and other sailors returning to their ships. Some went down the stairs and trekked up the rocky coast toward the dock that supported the barge we'd arrived on and where Jerek's and three other riverboats waited. Inside the narrow stone streets, we passed several shops. My stomach rumbled at the smell wafting over from an eatery on my right. Several tables with patrons littered the walk before the building in which someone grilled meat. But the odor of dead fish assaulted me from the left and replaced any signs of hunger. I turned toward the offensive smell to see a wiry man rushing out from behind a wet and bloody table. He had a silver and yellow fish by the tail, blood dripping onto the stones. He scurried across the street to the eatery that had smelled so wonderfully before. We pressed on.

I followed for another hundred paces or so, stretching my stride again in an attempt to maintain pace with the men. With their longer strides, they'd distanced themselves from me by ten paces. The crowd was loose enough that I could easily catch up with a few skip-steps, but lingering seemed of little harm. One merchant drew my attention. He haggled with an older man over a copper kettle and the merchant's table displayed a dozen other pieces forged from the metal . . . bowls, bracelets, and knobs. My focus fell little upon what he sold but more the clothing the man wore. Bloused pants, sandals, and a loose shirt with a vest—not terribly colorful, nonetheless fashioned in the Tsinti style. For a time, I lost myself, forgot that I strolled through cobbled streets in Kōkai, and felt the grasses of the Central Grasslands beneath my feet. During the mornings before the oxen moved, several men in Yankos's caravan had worked the golden orange metal over small fires. The work with copper hadn't seemed important then, but I smiled as another piece of the wandering folk clarified in my understanding. Under tsym, the Tsinti had never bartered with mon though they readily displayed it on their overskirts. I veered toward the merchant when a voice, so gentle I almost missed it, said from the shadows, "You'd do well to visit the gnoble in residence at the city's keep."

EIGHT

The Casteless

HALTING, I TURNED MY head, my brow furrowing. A cloak hid the owner of the voice, but there were no others around to whom she might have spoken. In my periphery, Thalaj spun, hand on his hilt, apparently having heard the meek suggestion as well. Perhaps his training with the Unseen allowed him to discern the quiet tone, or mayhap he'd taken note of her as he passed. The woman—no, a waif-like girl even under the cloak—stood against a wall. She pushed back the hood to reveal her smudged face. When the hood fell to her shoulders, I noted her hair hung in a messy braid, and wide, clear eyes regarded me as if she felt apprehensive about approaching us. Moving closer, I took more inventory of her appearance. Threadbare clothes. Small, dirty hands. A hole in the toe of her boot.

She seemed too young to be able to have worn the same boots long enough to wear a hole through the toe, and the space behind the hole was dark. Her feet didn't reach the end. Clearly she'd come by the boots after most of their life had been exhausted by another with much larger feet. She said no more as I moved into the shadows to meet her. Thalaj joined me, some of the gusto leaving his posture as he took in the nonthreatening sight. Hoaris trailed him but stayed closer to the street.

"Did you mention there's a gnoble present in the city?" I asked.

The girl gave a few tiny, jerking nods and wrung her hands.

"Who?" Thalaj snapped.

She flinched.

I held out both hands in an attempt to calm her. "May I have the name and caste?"

She backed away. Her voice mousy, she answered, "The Stone Lady, Sarangarel."

Thalaj and I shared a silent exchange.

I wasn't sure, first of how this girl would have known to approach us, and second how the Stone Singer gnoble would be able to help with our needs to sail across the Syrensea. But the small girl lifted her face with certainty and captured my full attention. Sarangarel would at least recognize Thalaj and me from the ascension ceremonies at the High Cloud Court. It followed to reason that she'd be willing to help the person she'd seen through ascension and called Kōgō in the days that followed.

Strangely, the girl's eyes shifted all about even though she seemed confident in having called to me and offering information. I gave her a smile in hopes I could reassure her further, let her know that we meant her no harm.

"May I have your name?" I asked, keeping my movements slow and my voice soft.

Thalaj placed a hand on my arm, a protective signal

to be cautious. When he stepped closer, the girl backed away again, pulling further into a shadowy alley between buildings.

"Truly, we don't wish to hurt you. I'm Mairy." I rested a hand over my chest, over the ever-heating and -cooling stones, and a haunting thought came to mind. Sarangarel. The Stone Lady. What if Stone Singers had been responsible for the stones that hung about my neck? Mayhap Thalaj's paranoia wasn't so misplaced after all. With her retreating, I had little time to worry over such puzzles, so I stowed the thought for later.

My first guard, also recognizing that he scared the girl more than I, tucked in behind me and whispered, "I'll stand with Hoaris. Find out if she can take us there." His voice quieted so only I could hear, cool breath at my ear, as he added, "And if she pulls a weapon, hold up a hand."

When he left, the girl relaxed a bit, the drawn features on her face smoothing and making her look five years younger. I smiled at her again. "What do others call you?"

"Honera," she whispered, her eyes dropping and then returning to mine.

"Honera," I repeated. "Thank you for signaling to us. How do you think Lady Sarangarel may help?"

"I-I can't be sure." She shook her head, but I waited patiently for her to continue—something I'd seen my father do on occasion when he tried to gain information from my sisters or me. Inevitably, one of us had felt the need to speak under the pressure of his gaze. The silence worked and she went on, "Along with her people, they're always looking for business."

I pursed my lips. How odd that a young girl would worry about such things. "Business? Of what sort?"

"They bring in lots of stone and gems from the rock fields to the east. They're always sending someone down to bargain with the ships, sometimes taking short jaunts out to sea. A moon back, they sent a crew of miners from the fields over to the Vesterisles. I just thought . . ." Honera twisted her fingers in front of her.

I pursed my lips and narrowed my eyes on the girl. Indeed, she'd been watching us since we'd dealt with the ships on the pier.

She fidgeted. "I-I'm sorry. Mayhap you search for something else."

"No, you did well. Thank you. But how did you know to choose us?" I asked.

The girl glanced behind her and shook her head when she focused back on me. "You have the lost look."

I could say the same of her. "*Honera* you said is your name?"

A nod.

"Well, I've never been to the City by the Sea. Can you guide us to the keep where Lady Sarangarel is in residence?"

Honera looked past me at Thalaj and Hoaris, then turned and looked down the alley behind her, but she still appeared uncertain.

I glanced back questioningly at Thalaj. His answering look urged me on. To the girl, I asked, "Will you allow my friend speak with us? He is my protector and seeing that you intend me no harm, he has no cause to hurt you either."

Again, she flinched, still twisting her fingers. Her eyes were wide, but she nodded yes. Thalaj approached when I waved him over. He moved cautiously behind me

130

and said, "I have two mons for you. One now and one after you show us where to find the gnoble."

Honera pressed her lips together and extended her fist. At full arm's length, she unfurled her fingers. Everything about her stance said, *Well and so, but do not come closer.* Heavy black lines shone from under her broken nails, and grime painted every crease of her revealed palm. Thalaj passed me an iron mon which I placed lightly into her cupped hand. The dirt-stained fingers snatched it away, and she turned quickly, calling, "This way!" as she trotted down the small space between buildings.

I lost track of the twists and turns, hoped that Thalaj or Hoaris would have a better sense of our way back to the docks, but I stayed on her heels. Suddenly at the center of a long alleyway with stone walls rising on either side, Honera stopped and pressed her back against a wall. "Up there." She pointed. "Street rats aren't welcome. The Stone Singer guards push us away with their rock hammers. We try not to be seen around them."

When Thalaj stepped forward, clearly intending to head to the end and take a look, Honera stood boldly in front of him, hand extended. "I did my part," she demanded, not at all the timid thing she'd appeared before.

My first guard looked down at her. "So you did, young lady." He placed the second coin in her palm.

She scampered back down the road but took a left where the cobbled streets formed a T instead of the right that would have retraced our path.

With only a small flit of his gaze to the scampering girl, Thalaj said to Hoaris, "You stay here with Mairynne. I'll take a look." He climbed the remaining paces to the top of the hill and turned the corner. After only a few seconds, he returned. "The gates to the house itself are well guarded. The guards refused my entry on the premise I had no appointment with the Stone Lady."

Lifting my chin, I said, "Did you ask in the name of the empress?" I despised that I found need to use my position, but speaking with Sarangarel felt necessary. In truth, Thalaj, though his father had been Frost Fighter and his mother Storm Sorcerer, outranked anyone within the Stone Singer caste. Yet I had enough trouble using my own position, and knowing how my guard viewed his station of mixed blood, I resisted mention. Focusing on mine instead, I added, "As kōgō, I hold higher caste rank than anyone here. It seems they'd be willing to show me directly to Lady Sarangarel upon my command."

Thalaj rubbed his chin. "Neither you nor I possess knowledge of aught that may have passed in Stormskeep. You disrobed yourself of the title when we set out on this journey. And in this case, it could very well pay to our advantage to assume the worst."

Hoaris grunted. "Doesn't hurt to just ask. Let me try." He started for the keep.

I smirked to my guard, cocking a brow.

Snatching him by the sleeve, Thalaj said, "Do you really think the Stone Singer guards will accept a Frost Fighter into their fortress?"

"We're not at constant war with them like the Fire Forgers and that tyrant of a leader, Atith."

Their gazes locked, each challenging the other, until without grace, Hoaris shrugged. "Guess we'll see; I'm going in. But in case it doesn't work, we might need to find a way to get a message delivered."

Thalaj rubbed the back of his neck. "I'll get the girl back. She won't take a message herself, but street rats know the city and will do just about anything for mon. As should be apparent by her quick change in attitude. Had she been quicker of hand, she might have slipped our purses."

The men nodded to one another, a plan and backup plan in play. Hoaris left in the direction of the guards.

To me, Thalaj said, "You wait here. I'll only be a few minutes."

As he went and I remained in the alley alone, my senses went on high alert. I strained to listen for their steps. Hoaris's fell heavily, but Thalaj made no sound. I backed up toward the wall, rested my hands against the rough stone, and tried to meld with my surroundings. My success in this endeavor felt meager. Any passerby would have recognized my awkward presence. Fortunately, none passed.

A few minutes trickled away, and my leg began to twitch; my breathing grew shallow. Worry seized me as I looked from one end of the alley to the other, but still, no one appeared. After another several long moments, a rustle came from the direction Thalaj had traveled. I stopped breathing. No voice reached my ears, but by the sound, people struggled nearby. I dropped a hand under my travel cloak to the hilt of a scimityne, feeling more confident with the blades after the season we'd spent with the Tsinti. I held my other hand outward, palm up and ready to gather the storm within.

◇◇◇◇◇◇◇◇

THE ENERGY I DREW fizzled as Thalaj came into view dragging a kicking and thrashing Honera down the alley. For reasons I couldn't reconcile, she didn't scream or cry out. Mayhap that was the way of the casteless in Kōkai. Would a cry for help bring the opposite? A glance over my shoulder told me we were still alone, and I sighed, relieved it was only him.

Clear exasperation on his face twisted his mouth, and I stifled a chuckle at seeing him so.

The girl made herself as heavy as possible while wriggling to get free and prying at his fingers. Then, she started grumbling. "I did what you asked. Let me go." Though still hushed, her tone grew panicked the nearer she drew. "You have no right! We're getting too close. They'll shred me!"

When he reached me, Thalaj huffed, grabbed her under both arms, and placed her on her feet facing me. In her fit, she didn't see me and continued to flail.

Reaching past her clawing hands, I grasped onto her upper arms. "Honera," I snapped.

She stopped, opening her eyes frenetically and looking around like trapped prey.

"Honera," I insisted, dodging to catch her shifting gaze. When her eyes finally rested on mine, I added, "We're not asking you to go in there. Settle yourself."

The girl turned her head one way then the other, searching for what I couldn't tell. Had my anxiety over being alone in the streets seemed stifling, hers spoke of certain fear for her safety. I wondered if she feared more than the Stone Singer guards.

"Look," Honera snapped, "I had a job to do and they're waiting on me."

"Who?" I asked.

She jerked her head around again.

I held tighter onto her grungy sleeves, shaking her once. "Who, Honera? Who is waiting on you?"

That silenced her. She definitely feared someone—or perhaps protected them. When I lifted my gaze to connect with Thalaj, the look he wore stated he clearly believed the same.

Breathing measured breaths, I urged her again. "As I said before, we mean you no harm."

"Then why is your brute holding me like this?" She shrugged, trying to pull herself from our shared hold.

I tightened my grip, considering how this version of the casteless girl behaved far bolder than she should. Tougher, too. She was too young to be so hard. What could have possibly brought her to this way of life? Not for the first time, I wondered about her parents and where she lived. Was she orphaned? And it rang strangely to my ears to hear her refer to Thalaj as a brute. I'd never seen him as anything other than safety, but now that I looked at his hard-lined jaw and broad shoulders, I had to admit she had a point. To anyone he didn't swear protection, he certainly would appear deadly.

Heavy footsteps from the end of the alley halted my words before I could reply. Hoaris trotted downhill over the cobblestones, pack bounding on his back, and he held his scabbard so that it wouldn't interfere with his run.

Honera tensed in my grasp; Thalaj tightened his hold. The big man wore his thoughts in the way he carried his head, shoulders, and brow, and I could read him without words. He'd had no luck with the guards.

I turned back to Honera who'd begun to writhe again. "Shhh. We need your help again, please."

"I'd no permission to *help* you before," she sneered.

Thalaj repositioned her so he had her about the waist within one arm. She kicked.

Hoaris stepped forward, addressing the girl freely now. "Why? Who said you couldn't help us?"

The girl pressed her lips together as if to hold back the words by force, but her resistance seemed to wane as the three of us pressed her.

I glanced around, hopeful others wouldn't witness the three of us holding tight to a smaller person while she thrashed for her freedom. Yet we needed her cooperation. Time to try one more time. "If my friend lets you go, can we talk? Will you stay and hear us out?"

Her nervous look cut between the three of us, then she jerked a nod.

I sighed and motioned for Thalaj to release her. She stood closest to the wall with the three of us surrounding her—still a threatening formation. She wouldn't make it very far if she tried to bolt between us. By the Triad's grace, she didn't. She straightened her shirt and turned her head, cracking her neck.

I started again, "We need to get inside to meet with Lady Sarangarel."

"To be sure; that's what I told you before," Honera said, folding her arms and jutting a hip.

I fought to keep reason in my tone. "The problem is that they aren't willing to simply allow us inside at our request."

"How is this my worry?"

Through gritted teeth, I continued, "We need someone to carry a message inside."

Honera held up her hands and shook her head vigorously. "Uh-uh. No. I told you before; they'll shred me."

But behind the action, in her eyes, there was something more. Mirroring her motion, I held up my hands too. "We're willing to pay if you have another idea of how we can either get her a message or get inside unnoticed." I raised my brows, waiting hopefully to see if she'd accept the bait of more mon.

Slowly, more softly, she said, "You got the wrong girl for that," and turned her eyes toward the gutter.

"But you have another idea?" I coaxed.

Reluctantly, she groaned, rolled her eyes, and held out her hand expectantly. "Filtch is going to hang me."

◇◇◇◇◇◇◇◇

AGAIN, WE WOUND THROUGH the narrow streets, heading in a direction that seemed dingier, less populated, and with more crumbling buildings. The doors often hung in shambles, some fastened by chains with heavy locks, others were just splintered wood that looked like they might fall apart if you pushed on them. I looked toward the roofs occasionally, at many of the stone walls collapsing from ill-repair. We moved at an easy pace through the streets. I walked beside Honera with little conversation, but she held us back at every corner and peered up and down the crossing passage before moving forward. The action seemed curious as I would have expected more threat from one of the buildings falling down upon us than from the open street. But she lived here and now offered her cooperation, so I followed her lead.

Several turns later, she pushed through one of the decrepit doors—one missing a chain. Honera went first, I followed, then Hoaris, and Thalaj pulled up the rear, keeping an eye over his shoulder at all times. She led us down a long hall, up two sets of stairs, and down another corridor before she turned into a room at the end, the precariously hung door open and awaiting our entry. Before going inside, I looked to my companions for guidance.

Thalaj shrugged one shoulder and touched the door. It issued a creak with little movement. "Can't be a trap. This door wouldn't hold a youngling, even before the babe learned to walk."

Inside, we climbed a set of worn stairs, followed down another hall, and crossed another threshold to our left. The only furnishing was a large square table with four benches, every surface scratched, pocked, and scarred as if someone had marked the wood with a knife. The walls had cracked and fallen in places, leaving piles of rubble in the corners, and the only light came from a small paneless window.

I held out my arms expectantly. "Where's this Filtch person?"

"Oh, he's not here." In a repeat of her stance in the alley, Honera jutted a hip, arms folded over her chest.

Cold anger rolled off Thalaj as he let out a huff and folded his arms as well. "Then why are *we* here?"

"My friends will be here soon. Getting in with Filtch takes a bit of work."

Her words only barely foreshadowed footsteps approaching from down the hall. Thalaj's hands drifted to the hilts of his daggers and Hoaris's to his sword as two boys, thin and dirty like our little guide but at the threshold of manhood, strode into the room. Assaying little threat, Thalaj and Hoaris eased their stances. The boys appeared more alarmed than Honera and shifted wary glances around the room.

Honera skipped over. The taller of the two grasped her

arm and pulled her into the corner to talk. I watched her hand over the iron mons we'd given her and wondered if this was Filtch. Even though I strained my ears, I couldn't hear more than whispers. Clearly having agreed to something, the taller boy called over the shorter one and then . . . they both left.

I lurched forward. "Where are they going?"

"Oh." Honera shrugged and sat at the table, seeming far less feeble than she'd been in the alley. "Just downstairs. They'll be back in a quick."

"And who are *they*?" I took a seat on another of the benches.

"We call 'em Gnat and Flea." She drew her brows together. "Not sure what their real names are." And that didn't seem to bother her as she crossed to the table, took a seat, and traced the engravings with her dirt-encrusted thumbnail.

Indeed, only a few moments passed before the footsteps came again down the hall, slower this time. When the boys appeared, the taller one handed Honera a plate of steaming food. It looked and smelled like some variety of stewed meat, and my stomach growled.

"Thanks," she said and took a bite of the bread from the plate. With a full mouth, she introduced us.

Flea, the shorter one, tossed an apple to each of us. It wasn't as hearty as the girl's meal, but it was whole, and the peel seemed intact.

Gnat said, "We didn't think you'd eat cooked food from us. You look smarter than that."

I thought of the golems in my pack, but we only had the two. Hoaris would still be at risk. Regardless, they didn't know of our little animated friends, so the assumption seemed sound.

Gnat walked to the window. "The fruit's from the tree there." He pointed.

Thalaj went to look, nodded, then wiped the peel on his shirt. He took a healthy bite, the crunch filling the silence. I grinned and did the same, sweeping away a trail of sugary juice that ran down my chin. It was a tiny pleasure, but I chewed and got lost in the sweet moment.

The tall boy leaned against the window, arms folded and shoulder slumped to one side. "Filtch will only see the girl, and not until sunset."

"Not an option." Thalaj gave no time for Gnat to continue or for anyone else to reply, and his words were finite.

I'd seen him exert that command before, but then didn't seem the time. "Thalaj," I said softly.

He raised his dark eyes to me. "No, Mairy. I'm not leaving your side. Remember what I told you in the cave at Safaia? My sworn duty."

Gnat stood, arms spread. "Then, I believe we're at an impasse."

Standing, I went to Thalaj and placed both hands on his arm. "Do you have a better idea?"

Thalaj simmered but remained silent. He looked warningly at the boys and at Honera, who chewed her food eagerly while we discussed. Hoaris stood to the side and ate his apple while he watched and waited for the next move.

I turned to the trio. "Can we have a few minutes alone?"

"Certainly," Gnat said, and they left, shuffling heels

across the dusty floor.

Honera stood with her plate and followed, still chewing.

When only the three of us remained, Thalaj spun to me. "Mairynne, there is no way I can leave you to go into some stranger's domain alone. You know that. You know it would break my vow to your family in the worst way."

I tucked my chin. His accusation rang true. What I asked was a violation of his pledge, but this seemed to warrant it. I couldn't remain passive here when I could possibly gain us another step in Father's direction. For reasons I couldn't name, I didn't see the same danger as he. Mayhap my guard's intuition stemmed from his training or his intent to pose the danger himself. Possibly I remained the naïve little princess who'd never ventured from her father's home, but I had it in my mind that all would be well. The stones about my neck remained even in temperature, not offering indication one way or the other. When I looked back up, I said as much, pulling back my cloak to reveal my scimitynes and adding, ". . . and between Yankos, Jorani, Baldeo, and you, I have been well trained in how to use these."

Thalaj eyed me skeptically. "You're only beginning to learn how to use those."

Hoaris bellowed a laugh from the other side of the room, distracting us both from our debate. As we turned, I could only imagine the twin questioning looks he saw. With another guffaw, he said, "You two bicker like my gram and pop. She'll probably be fine, Thal. It's just another of the casteless."

My cheeks felt hot at the comparison to an old married pair, but his reassurance pleased me nonetheless.

"None of the casteless have been much of a threat."

Hoaris took a final huge bite of the apple and chewed. "Skinny street rats and not much more. Send her in with a few mon, and she'll be back before you know it."

I turned back to my guard. "Well and so, and I've rested enough on the barge and haven't used the elementals in days. If needed, I can call upon the storm. All it would take is a single burst of lightning and I can be free." That wasn't something I could do often, and the act drained my energy like no other usage of the magic inherent to my people. But I could call it if I were short on options and had access to the skies. With the state of the windows in these buildings, I didn't see that as an issue either.

Thalaj pursed his lips. Then he rubbed his normally smooth chin, but because he hadn't shaved in days, the motion issued a rasping sound. His eyes shifted and he worked his lips a little more as thoughts ran behind his eyes. Then, he relented. He went to the door and motioned to the three casteless who'd likely eavesdropped the entire time.

With everyone inside again, Thalaj said, "Well and so. She'll go with you at sundown. I'll return to the market in the meantime. Hoaris, can we have a word outside before I take leave?"

My jaw gaped. Though I'd all but demanded I go, I hadn't expected him to leave me there to wait for Otarr to retire for the day. I also didn't hear what passed between the men in murmur outside the door, but I trusted Thalaj. Zofi's counsel echoed: *He will always be there for you. There will come a time when you'll doubt but rest easy as he will always return.* I reminded myself of that and gave him the space to seek whatever he needed at the market. With the boys and Honera, I took a seat, awkward silence hanging heavy within the room.

Hoaris returned with a wide grin and heavy step,

and flounced onto the bench across the table. He pulled out a small purse and looked questioningly at the three younglings. "Dice?"

None of the three knew how to play, so Hoaris explained the simplistic rules to Gnat, Flea, and Honera the same way he'd explained it to me on the barge. I listened to him, ineptly craving an answer to what had transpired between him and Thalaj in the hall. But alas, I had resolved myself to trust my guard.

We played for hours, using the seeds from the apples we'd eaten as pretend mon. Hoaris, of course, won time and time again. After each victory, he'd redistribute the seeds and we'd start anew. By late afternoon, Gnat was getting pretty good. He bested Hoaris twice before light footsteps in the hall approached, and Hoaris swept the dice into his pouch.

A woman appeared in the doorway dressed in simple gray, but her attire was clean. Distaste wriggled upon her lips as she peered around the room and its dilapidated condition. She looked down a long nose at the five of us sitting around the table. Hoaris stood, but she walked straight past him and stared at Honera. "He'll deal with *you* tomorrow." Then to me, she held out a heavy cloth blindfold and said, "Filtch awaits your company. My *lady*."

NINE

Filtch, Patron of the Casteless

HONERA SHRANK UNDER THE woman's haughty words and anger flared inside me at the way she looked at and talked to the girl. It mattered little in my view how low Honera was in terms of caste or class, she remained a person. Though I owned the most authority in Nantai, I hadn't considered approaching anyone of the casteless in such a superior manner.

"What gives you authority to treat others so?" The words flew from my lips before I'd considered their weight, before I remembered that I wasn't the empress here. Despite that, I felt justified in the question and pushed my chin higher as I stood from my seat. "And who are you?"

She'd seemed larger while I sat—possibly from the air of supremacy she held about her—but standing, I looked down to meet her eyes, ignoring the swath of material in her hand.

She didn't answer my questions but looked coolly at Gnat. "Since you didn't return with word otherwise, I thought she'd agreed to Filtch's conditions." Her hand holding the blindfold dropped to her side.

"What conditions?" I asked. "The only condition shared was that I go alone, without Hoaris or Thalaj."

The woman's glare shifted to me. "You brought a petition to us. If you wish to speak with Filtch, you will come with me now, alone *and* blindfolded."

Hoaris pounded a heavy fist on the table, the dice rattling. The bench scraped the floor, and the temperature in the room dropped suddenly as the mountainous man stood. "No one spoke of blindfolds. That implies prisoner."

The clamor didn't seem to influence the woman. She simply looked up at Hoaris as if she had grown tired of the conversation. "You'll understand that our master wishes to retain his anonymity. We have not bound her and only expect she follow without sight. These are the terms, Filtch's offer of his service, if you will. If they aren't to your liking, we can close the deal now and I can be about more important business." She lifted a brow.

I tapped my foot through a pause where all eyes in the room turned in my direction. Seeing little alternative, I leaned across the table toward Hoaris. "You went to the guards. Do you think there's another way to reach Sarangarel? Do you think there's another way to secure our passage with the mons we have?"

The manner in which he dropped his eyes told me he had naught but doubts regarding our odds.

"Filtch can help you, I am certain," the woman interrupted, any inflection absent from her voice. "Although, I haven't all night to await your decision."

I reached for the stones under my tunic, pressing

them against my chest to see if they offered any guidance, any flare of cold or hot, something to make accepting the risk more palatable. Once again, they remained at an even temperature. My shoulders sagged. Apparently, the spell cast upon them only reassured me when I questioned my path, reasserting in the conviction that I must find my father. Precisely *how* I went about the task, they would leave to my discretion. Zofi had warned that time was of import to Father, that he could only persist in "stasis" for so long.

Stasis. Another concept beyond my understanding. Yet in that moment within the rundown room, Father's uncertain time and future drove my answer.

"Very well." I sighed.

Victory danced in her icy-blue eyes. "You can leave your pack here with your friend." She pulled the cloth through her hands and reached to tie it around my head.

I pushed my traveling bag toward Hoaris, grateful she hadn't asked me to divest myself of my weapons or the purse I carried on my belt.

I'd never seen him aught but jovial, but now he shot me a wary look. "I-I'm not so sure about this. Th—" He pressed his lips together, then restarted. "Your protector will see that my throat yawns if anything happens to you."

The woman said, "Rest assured, we mean her no harm. This is only for our protection. She will return before dawn."

"Give me a moment," I said to the woman. Rounding the end of the table, I rested a hand on his arm. "Unless you have another idea, I must."

Even through his beard, a muscle jumped visibly in

his jawline. He gave a small nod. "If you're not back at first light, we'll tear the city apart," he said to me, his eyes fixated on the woman. "And I'll have your name before you may take her."

Again, she jutted her chin higher. "You may call me Wren."

"That's it? Wren?" Hoaris boomed.

I pulled at his arm. "It's enough.

After he had settled, I said to Wren, "Shall we?" I turned my back, vulnerable and hoping that her words rang true, that she and her master intended only aid and information, as she secured the black material in place.

Night had been falling before. The room had been in shadows.

Now, it was black.

Wren took my arm at the elbow and guided me away. We walked slowly and with little conversation aside from small instructions on where to place my feet. Through the door and hall, down the stairs and the lower hall, then we stepped outside. The air on my face felt fresher, more alive, and I took note of the difference. Several counted turns later, we entered another building, the air once again stale. Throughout this all, Wren made no remark beyond *step up, step down, right, left, . . .* Inside, we climbed six runs of stairs. I breathed hard by the time we stopped, and I listened for her to do the same. Nothing. Had she called upon some assistance from the elements to aid her journey? There'd been no wind, cold, or heat. Mayhap she'd simply trained her body to climb so quickly. The pressure on my arm hinted at her reach toward something ahead, and a door creaked. We moved forward again, the enlivened air hitting my forehead, nose, and chin once again; outside then. On a roof, I imagined.

At another twenty paces, Wren said, "Climb again," and we scaled another run of twelve stairs. She pulled me along, not seeming to go in any particular direction, and after much wandering, she stopped and reached again. This time, no door creaked, but then she urged me forward another dozen steps and drew to a halt, at last releasing my arm. Someone—*Wren?*—worried at the knot and the blindfold fell away.

The room in which I stood wasn't much larger than the decrepit room where we had spent the day playing dice with the casteless—Gnat, Flea, and Honera. It was clean and boasted decorations, a clear display of affluence. A carved wooden desk, three chairs with scrolled backs and arms, and a cushioned seating area furnished the space. There were many shelves lining the side walls, and each supported clusters of candles or a candelabra to provide light. Behind the lit and flickering tapered candles, mirrors reflected each flame's amber glow to make the room seem brighter still. At a hearth, a figure stood gazing upon the fire. I drew my brows to a peak as I, too, peered at the fire. It glowed and danced like any other, but it didn't put off smoke. There was no chimney, and the stone around it didn't show signs of char. Yet the flames flickered. And for all the fire within the gray stone room, the temperature remained cool.

Wren crossed to the figure by the fire—Filtch, I presumed—bowed her head, then left us. I followed her path, taking note of the intricately carved double doors she closed behind her. So at odds with every other building we'd passed earlier in the day. I faced the stranger—long, thin, and plain in appearance, Filtch wore clothing fitted to his form, clothes like none I'd seen before, light in color with no material sagging or flowing as was customary among the Nantai people. He wore his hair trimmed close to his head, also unlike our customs. When he turned,

I took in his smooth, too-faultless complexion. Eyes, brows, nose, mouth, and chin, all balanced in a way that suggested a portrait rather than a person.

In a voice equally as flawless, he said, "Evangale, the youngest *once*-empress of the Nantai people, it is truly my pleasure to meet you again."

◇◇◇◇◇◇◇◇

THERE I STOOD. IN a room seemingly having no place in the City by the Sea, I gaped at the pristine person before me, ageless to my eyes as if he'd been sculpted rather than born. Confusion danced through my mind. He should only recognize me if he had spent time in Arashi at Stormskeep. And then only if he'd seen me in an occasion of less formality or growing up when I was freer to dress casually and wear my hair free as I desired. Even as I'd approached my majority, my mother, Kōgō Noralynne, as part of her royal duties, and Mother Feathergale had been grooming me to look the part of an empress. When Father had written me into the annals as his heir, their ministrations had only intensified.

But this young man before me would know nothing of those times. "How is it—Filtch, is it?" I waited for him to nod his assent, then continued, "that you know me, but I don't believe we've met before this moment."

Filtch moved to the desk, took a seat, and flourished an arm across the tabletop toward a chair.

I hesitated, but in the end, I'd gone blindfolded with Wren to see this man who offered a sliver of hope in getting a message into Lady Sarangarel's grasp. One of my hands covered the small pouch at my belt, and the other felt for the hilt of a scimityne. Reassured by the presence of the weapons, I sat on the edge of a chair and rolled my shoulders back to lengthen my spine. "Will you honor me with an answer to my questions as well?"

Filtch reclined in his chair, folding his fingers together under his chin. "I understand that this is difficult for you, but it matters little to me that you don't recognize me from your past experience. Although, if you search, you might find a way to discover my true identity.

"Regardless, that is of little importance. We're here to see what I might do for you, is that true?" He smirked.

Yes, he'd posed the important question, but the other niggled under my skin. I couldn't place him. Regardless, I shifted in the chair to move the weapons so I could settle back for the conversation in the same manner he clearly had. "I understand that you might be able to get a message delivered for me."

"I have many messengers. To whom do you need to send this message?" He sat utterly motionless, his eyes boring into me as he spoke.

Honera had known our plight, suggested it even, so I hesitated. Wasn't he the patron of the casteless? Slowly, I answered. "The Gnoble Lady Sarangarel."

He spread graceful fingers to either side. "And what possible favor could you have to beg of one *four* castes below your own?"

Again, Filtch stilled, but I sensed disdain in the sharp edge in his words. I narrowed my eyes, trying to infer his intent. The casteless, the *rats* as Honera had pointed out, would care little of the upper caste machinations. So why was it that a leader within the casteless of Kōkai would worry about me stooping beneath my ranks? His worry hinted that he had more involvement with caste politics, that he was someone more than what he appeared.

I cleared my throat. "You'll forgive me, but since you

know my position within Nantai society, you'll also be informed the topic of caste is one I'd only discuss with advisers and those sitting upon the Gnoble Council."

Again, he gave a small and superior smile. "And, Lady Mairynne, you will also forgive my impropriety, but I believe you are the one in need here." He folded his hands once more, as if to close that part of the discussion and iterate my obvious position in this conversation.

Clearly, there were no others present or begging his help.

We stood at an impasse, each unwilling to meet on middle ground. This matter wouldn't succumb to negotiation or haggling. Given the comfort of the office where we presently sat, he wasn't a street rat in need of mon. Were that so, I would offer my purse. Though he possessed the information I required, Filtch clearly would offer nothing more while I refused him such discussion. Yet I found myself unwilling to put our plight at a further disadvantage by divulging more than truly necessary. In faith alone, I'd risked leaving my companions and going with Wren, and it seemed a possible mistake.

I placed my hands on the chair's arms and pushed to my feet. "Well, I must thank you for the time, but it appears another solution will be necessary. Can you ask Wren to return and see me back to my friends?"

Filtch closed his eyes and took several measured breaths. At length, he stood too. "Wait." He stepped away from the chair and closer to the cool fire in the hearth.

Mayhap he possessed a version of the Frost Fighters' sorcery, for I still couldn't believe the fire before me.

He held his hands clasped in front of him and turned in a slow circle. When his back faced me, his head lolled forward and his body shimmered, grew transparent like mist. It reformed as he completed his revolution. Completing a full rotation, he raised a neither feminine nor masculine face to meet my watching gaze.

I hissed air in through my teeth, eyes wide, and my hand covered my mouth as the emblem stared at me. Upon the shoulder . . . a swan.

The Swan.

"I believe this is the face and attire you will recognize," said the Cloud Courtier, Alto-Trea, and reversed the slow circle, reassuming the clean and simple visage of Filtch.

Throat tight, silenced, and insides heaving, I sank back into the chair. Filtch took his seat too as I searched for words. So much had been amiss about the path to this room and about the room itself. It had seemed too nice to exist within such a rundown area of Kōkai. We hadn't traveled far enough to reach another district. That meant—

"We are within a cloud castle," I said, all hope having fled.

Mists in the darkness within the Yubar . . .

The cloud that had lingered over Safaia . . .

Filtch, a person who'd followed us from Arashi, issued a single nod, his fingers steepled at his chin.

I turned to the door, my heart pounding furiously in my ears, then looked back at Alto-Trea—no, Filtch, or—

By the sacred Triad, I didn't know what to think. One thing I held certain: Thalaj wouldn't rest if they failed to return me safely. The room about me wasn't the airy version of the castle at the High Cloud Court. Even in the amber glow of the flame, it held a heavy grayness, like a storm cloud ready to empty over the earth.

"We are still within the city. You have naught to fear." Filtch's tone was one that seemed wont to calm my anxiety or maybe belittle my worry, but just as easily as he'd tried to allay my fear, he added, "Yet."

"What interest do you have in the casteless of this city?" My skin prickled, outrage balling inside my stomach. Though I feared for myself, I still worried over the people. "Why do you so disguise yourself? Do they know you're a Courtier?" A hundred other questions boiled in my mind, but those were the only ones that would surface in the maelstrom as I attempted to trace the Cloud Courtier's motives.

"Ahh, young Evangale, you begin to piece things together. I have shared my true identity with you, and I trust that you'll keep that information between us. Will you now share your reasons for seeking the assistance of Sarangarel?"

I noted the absence of her gnoble title but gritted my teeth. Another small, albeit carefully played slight prodded at my patience. However, my need to know if he could—or *would*—help gained urgency. "I seek to charter passage across the Syrensea."

"Oh, truly?" Filtch tilted his head, interest the first apparent emotion I could recall written upon his face since having entered this room.

"Truly."

"And what is your destination?"

"How is that of import to my request of you? I merely need you to help with delivering a missive to the *Lady*." I measured my voice, carefully emphasizing the title.

"Well stated . . . *Lady Mairynne*."

I lifted a brow. "I believe the address you're searching

for would be *Kōgō*."

He smiled. "Might I offer some fire-flower wine?"

My mouth flooded at the mention of the cordial I hadn't tasted since my departure from Stormskeep, but I hadn't brought my taster. The golem remained in my pack with Hoaris. Steeling myself for more courtly banter, I smiled as sweetly as possible. "That would be pleasing. But would you mind terribly if I asked you to drink from my glass before I partake?" *He* would do equally as well as my little animated self.

Filtch contemplated for a long moment, certainly rolling around my accusation in his mind. Then he stood and went to the door. When he returned, he had two of the bubbling glasses in hand. He sipped from each and handed me one. "This is a rare pleasure that you don't experience when traveling afoot, I presume." He sighed. "I cannot fathom the unpleasantries of sleeping upon the ground. I lost you for a time after the night we last spoke, but having a sky island helps in navigating Nantai, you see." He sipped again.

I took a drink; the bubbles danced on my tongue, and I longed for the keep where I'd grown to my majority, where my family remained, where I knew every turn, and where I felt safe. Indeed, my body ached from the travel and a part of me yearned for the comforts lost.

Home.

But as I swallowed, the stones flared around my neck. One hot, the other cold. Despite the wine's simple pleasure and the reminder of what I'd sacrificed, my path ahead would veer away from my lands and my people, ". . . *over the Syrensea to the island nation of Ise, and inland still*," Zofi had foretold.

"Thank you for the wine, Filtch." I placed my almost

empty glass on his desk. "You are being a most wonderful host. However, I wonder if we might return to my purpose? My friends await."

"Ah, speaking of your friends, to where has your loyal first guard disappeared?"

"To tell you the truth, I do not know." And for the time I was glad that Thalaj had only spoken to Hoaris. "I believe he went to the markets, but he didn't share his purpose or destination."

"Do you know when he will return."

It cut that I hadn't that knowledge either. I lifted my chin. "Our understanding of this little arrangement was that I'd be back before dawn, so I'd assume he will return to the building before Selene has finished her night's journey." I paused, again feeling that the trajectory of the conversation meandered. "So, you will understand my need to conclude our business in a prompt manner."

"I do understand, Lady."

Again, the ill-address rankled, but I measured my breathing and held my tongue. Kōgō had never been a status I'd wanted but somehow, as this disguised courtier kept using a lesser title, anger stirred from the depths of my soul.

Filtch drained his wine. "You inquired before why I had interest in the casteless, Lady Mairynne. I do have a certain fondness for simplicity." He seemed far away as he spoke, but then shook off wherever his mind had wandered. "I must say, though, it is not only the casteless within the City by the Sea that I take interest in."

"I fail to follow." I blinked several times, feeling something had fallen into my eye and clouded my vision.

"Are you aware that there is a large purse, strings

upon strings of bronze mon, offered for your return to Stormskeep?"

"Why would it surprise me that my aunt and sisters would offer a prize to have me returned safely?" I answered without hesitation.

Filtch folded his fingers and reclined again. "You misunderstand my meaning."

Again, I tried to relax into the chair, a solid attempt to maintain control. "Then I presume you will enlighten me?"

"There is a price for both you *and* Thalaj Northerngale."

This news was a bit unexpected, but as Thalaj had been our father's protector before mine, it wouldn't be an entirely absurd notion. "You've still told me nothing that would be cause for alarm."

"As I said, I take interest in the casteless within multiple cities. Arashi is one, and the messenger network is a particular interest of mine."

I tensed. Hoaris had mentioned that someone had ordered the Stormskeep gates sealed. Naturally, they would put out word beyond the walls if they were offering a reward for my return. But his words suggested that he had connections inside.

Filtch went on, "There is a new empress sitting on the Serpentine Throne."

I'd decreed that Nadia would take my place in the interim. "This is as I expected. I couldn't leave without appointing another to the duty."

He spread his hands, then refolded his fingers. A smokeless flame flickered in his eyes. "Once again, you misread my intentions."

"Then would you state it plainly?" I snapped, losing my careful control within, but I maintained my poised posture.

Filtch tsked. "We have had quite the uncommon number of ascension ceremonies in recent times. It gives my people in the clouds quite the purpose, you see. We thrive upon our courtly duties, so we are more than happy to accommodate."

Frustratingly, he dallied. I sat there as calm as possible while a current ran through my blood and my muscles twitched in anticipation of flying into action. I toyed with the hem on my cloak, rubbing the rough stitches with my thumb as the only outlet for my growing frustration.

A grin split Filtch's face. "Shortly after you disappeared, your aunt, Nadialynne Riversgale, completed the rituals. Our production of 'The Spirit Sosano, the Blooming Princess, and the Regalia of the Nantai,' I must admit, was one of our finest. But I do believe the one following your sister's ascension will be written about in songs."

"What?" Standing abruptly, I launched toward the table, leaned closer to Filtch on both arms, and spewed forth shocked question after shocked question. "My sister's ascension? How is that possible? Nadia would have never decreed such a thing. Which sister? Certainly not Yasmynne! So . . ."

"Yesss," Filtch hissed, "Your logic is true. Kōgō Karynne Evangale is the sitting empress of Nantai. So you see, it would not have been appropriate for me to call you Kōgō."

Karynne, my loving but strong-willed sister—the very sister who'd proclaimed to me before my ceremony that she was past her jealousy over our father having named me heir—had somehow figured a way to take the

Serpentine Throne for her own. I paced the small room in an arc, giving action at last to my coiled muscles. Filtch couldn't have had a hand in the situation, but how? Who? . . . and why? I grasped at the stones around my neck. Even through the material of my tunic, they flared hot and icy-cold. My parents expressed anger to me in the only way possible . . . from wherever their souls had traveled.

I hadn't a clue what action I should undertake next. Should I go home? The stones returned to normal within my hand. Should I continue on my current venture? Heat flared in my palm. I'd never been so certain of my father's presence near my heart, and despite the gut-wrenching spectrum of possible treachery, I knew beyond doubt . . . I must stay my course and follow the stones.

Throughout my pacing and puzzling, Filtch sat behind his desk with calm satisfaction, and I despised him for that. I wanted to lash out, to scream until my frustration had run its course, but that seemed a youngling's reaction. If anything, I needed to maintain a level of maturity and control. I stopped my pacing in front of the door. Turning to him, resolved, I said firmly, "I need to get that missive to Stone Lady Sarangarel. Can you help me or not? If you cannot, I will be on my way."

I yawned.

"Oh, but Lady, you've overlooked something."

Shaking my head, I demanded, "And what, pray tell, is that?" I held my hands in fists at my sides, resisting the urge to call the storm, but there were no windows. I had no connection to the skies or water. And then . . .

My arms grew heavy; my legs weakened.

"You've assumed that I *will* help you. Having such ability and exercising it are two entirely different prospects. Offering assistance to you and your guard would mean treason on my part." He lay a hand over his chest. "The notion of imprisonment within a spire at Stormskeep . . . well . . ." He shivered. "You see, that is not a fate I'm willing to endure."

The room darkened. I pressed my eyes wider open, fighting. "What have you given me?"

He flipped his hand, gracefully but dismissing my worry. "It was but a mild sedative."

"But . . . you drank . . . from my glass?" I stammered slowly.

"Ah, yes. The elixir is one I take on an almost nightly basis. I have trouble sleeping otherwise, you see. Honestly, I envy your intolerance." Filtch stood. "I'll have to drink another to find sleep tonight, I believe. Mayhap even a third." He walked around the desk.

The room spun as I tried to focus on him. Vaguely, I heard the door opening behind me as my knees gave way. The lights dimmed. Filtch caught me before I sank to the ground, and before I slept, I heard him say, "Find her a room for the night. We'll leave with the thinning morning fog."

TEN

The Escape

THE BED IN WHICH I awoke felt almost like my own with ample cushion, plump pillows, and a heavy blanket. I stretched as if that were true, but as soon as clear and conscious thought settled upon me, I sprung upright. Darkness hung thickly within the room, and though my eyes were wide, I couldn't see. Reaching for the wind, water, or charge in the air, I felt none, no connection to the sky. No windows, I concluded. My captor understood my sorcery's limitations well enough—as a Cloud Courtier would. I patted my chest, arms, and legs, breathing relief that I still wore my own tunic and pants. But my cloak, weapons, belt, purse, and boots were all no longer about my body. I squinted, blinked rapidly as if to clear a blur, but the blackness remained. I turned my head slowly this way and that to search out any sliver of light, but there was none. My chest constricted, and I sucked in a breath, holding it and hoping the tightness would relent.

Think, Mairynne. Think.

Filtch—what an appropriate moniker for the Swan. Alto-

Trea's reappearance and the conversation before I'd fallen to the elixir thundered through my mind. Each remembrance sizzled inside me as if each new fissure in my soul shot lightning through my core. Unfortunate, how it failed to produce a strike that might be used to free me from whatever prison in which I'd awoken. Feeling so torn and confused, I often would have summoned the rain, but when I had no connection to the skies or elements, I couldn't release the storm's magic..

My throat felt dry and my palms wet.

How had Karynne shifted the mantle of leadership from Nadia to herself? How had she convinced our sweet aunt? Or *had* she convinced her? Had Karynne forcibly usurped the Serpentine Throne and thereby . . . the price placed upon my head had little to do with her sisterly love? If she'd intended something aught, worse perhaps, I'd sorely misjudged her intent. If she'd sponsored an ill fate upon our aunt, what harm did she intend for me? Sealing the keep's gates was an action only taken in treacherous times, but Nantai wasn't at war. What danger could possibly exist for the residents of Stormskeep? Regardless, it seemed my sister or my aunt—or perhaps both—had betrayed my wishes.

I reached for my necklace, happy to find the stones in place. Then I touched the cuff on my upper arm beneath my sleeve. Still there. So they'd relieved me of my weapons and other accessories, but they hadn't searched me fully. Tsanseri had mentioned I may have need of the trinket one day, but what could that have meant? If she were here, would she act against Alto-Trea—one who'd participated in her audience within Love's Court when Yasmynne made her petition?

Huffing, I dropped my hand to my lap, regretful over not heeding my protector's warnings. Pushing the covers back, I swung my feet over the edge of the bed. The floor, cold and smooth even through my stockings, felt like the ones in the High Cloud Court. Standing, I kept a hand on the bed and stretched the other blindly before me. I took shuffling steps until I came to a wall. Feeling my way, I did the same along the wall. Strange that no furniture obscured my path. When I reached the corner, I turned. At three more paces, my thigh bumped the corner of a table. I explored. My frantic, trembling hands ran over the surface and below—no drawers, only a simple table— but on top, I found things. A belt. A purse. Rough-spun wool, folded neatly. *My* things? I fumbled to open the purse's clasp and feel inside. Coins, a few stones from the Stone Singers' gift at my ascension, and the mirror. I'd forgotten about the tiny circular mirror that should allow me to see things in their true form. How helpful that would have been upon my arrival . . . and something I should have used with Honera and the other casteless. I closed my eyes, rueful that such a thing had slipped my mind. Yet that particular object confirmed these were indeed my belongings.

Beside the table under darkness still, I donned the belt, purse, and my cloak, then I continued my slow journey-by-feel up and down the wall. On the floor beside the table, I kicked something and reached for it— my boots. The absence of sight also erased balance, so I sat to prevent toppling over, slipped my feet inside, and laced them. The only missing items were my weapons and scabbards. I groaned. What would Thalaj say when he discovered that I had lost the weapons he'd had crafted especially for me?

Keep searching, Mairynne. You don't know that you've lost them yet, I reminded myself.

I made it down the third wall, encountering no other furniture, and on the fourth, presumably on the opposite of the bed where I'd begun, I found the door. I tried the latch; it wouldn't give. I beat on the door, called out for help, pounded until my fist ached, then I pressed my ear close and listened.

Nothing.

For long, empty moments . . . only silence.

With my back against the wall beside the door, I sank to the floor, at a loss for what to do next other than wait. My last recollection within Filtch's office hadn't been more than two hours after dark. Without light or access to the skies and awakening from a drugged slumber, I couldn't guess if morning had arrived. I assumed Alto-Trea had tucked me into a room upon his sky island. The time was of more worry.

"Find her a room for the night. We'll leave with the thinning morning fog," Filtch had said as the elixir pulled me under.

Did that mean—?

I strained my ears and listened hard, tried to hear or feel the soft hum I recalled from my time at the High Cloud Court. Again—nothing. For all I knew, we could have departed from the City by the Sea and arrived somewhere else while I slept. Everything had turned into a youngling's game of guessing.

Aloud, I whispered, "Oh, Thalaj, I am so sorry I wouldn't listen." My head fell back to rest on the wall. Had I listened, I wondered if we would both be in my current predicament. Mayhap, but at least we'd be together.

After several long minutes there against the wall, I heard a series of small clicks, fumbled my way to standing, and held my arms wide, ready to call for my powers. If the door opened to a space where I could connect with the sky or a source of moisture, at least, I could call upon the storm's power and defend myself against whomever was there. I held my hand forward, ready.

The door swung inward; the soft light was bright enough that it pierced my eyes, yet night still kept the city in shadow. I squinted as my eyes adjusted, but no one stood in the opened door. Cautiously, I went forward, peering out to one side, then the other. The exit revealed an open space and the sprawling city beyond wisps of dark clouds. The room had blocked sound, but waves still crashed in the distance. I turned my head left, straining to hear more. A soft keening—akin to the sounds the blue dragon had made over Safaia.

I looked to my right for someone. Anyone. The skies remained dark from horizon to horizon. Selene still hung low above but would soon turn her watch over to Otarr and the light, but I had no way to know how much night remained. Beyond the few city lanterns still aglow, there was a vast darkness. The Syrensea. I reached toward the darkness to test my theory and could feel the moisture from the huge body of water gathering to answer my beckoning. I held tightly to the power as I searched for something or someone.

Who had opened the door?

I turned to the left where a hallway led into the castle. The keening came again—so much pain within the sound. It riveted my feet in place as my heart pulled in two different directions.

Where had the woman, Wren, brought me? How would I return to Hoaris and Thalaj? If I went toward the city, would I find cloud steps down? Who had opened the door?

Why did the dragon mourn? Did the Cloud Courtier hold her captive as he held me? Did she yearn for her freedom the same as I, or something more? Alone and out of imminent danger, I ruled out calling a storm as it would certainly set my captor on alert. I desperately wanted to find my scimitynes, if only for the security of having a weapon in my palm. But overall, that seemed less important than getting back to Thalaj and Hoaris.

Father's voice replayed in my mind, Truth to thine self first.

Zofi's then about Father, It is uncertain how long he can remain in stasis.

And hers about Thalaj, He will always be there for you. There will come a time when you'll doubt but rest easy as he will always return.

My heart broke for the dragon, but I needed to answer Father's call. Braced in the doorway, I looked both ways several more times, judging, trying to decide. How long did I have before first light? Attempting to help the dragon again wouldn't further my cause. I'd aided her once, but certainly she was stronger than Filtch and could care for herself this time. "I'm sorry," I whispered to her, my eyes burning. Unable to endanger myself further, I stepped through the door, the cool air raising the hairs on my arms, and started toward the city.

A croon sounded again from behind and halted my flight. I pivoted and jogged the other way—toward the sound.

"No!" a distant voice cried. Muffled. Familiar.

A jolt surged up my spine, halting me at the corner. I pressed my back to the wall and looked back toward the room where I'd been held captive. Kyr? I would have sworn that voice belonged to the Small Folk woman, but I saw nothing. My heart pounded in my throat, and I fought to control my breathing. Just my imagination, or mayhap Filtch's elixir caused more than sleep. I closed my eyes and inhaled. Ten. Exhaled. Nine. I opened my eyes; inhaled. Eight. By the time I reached five, I'd gained control and listened again for the dragon's sounds.

I might have missed it if I hadn't been concentrating, but the dragon's voice was still there, a soft and constant rumble punctuated occasionally with a higher-pitched whine. Then she emitted a louder wail that sounded hoarse as if she'd exhausted herself from the efforts. Then, it faded again to the low grumbling. I stayed close to the wall and peered around the corner, right then left.

I shrank into a low crouch when I caught sight of two people stood not more than fifty paces away engaged in hushed conversation. Both were dressed in attire of the people who dwelled in the Great Sands region that stretched from the eastern border of Nantai across the northern half of Yōtei. I'd only seen the clothes in illustration—loose pants that fit tight at the ankles, knee-length robes with long billowy sleeves, an ample scarf about the neck, and another draped over the head and affixed with a dark band around the crown. I could only see one of their faces, a young man whose olive skin, inky black hair, and lighter eyes reminded me of someone. At the distance, I couldn't tell his exact eye color, only that they weren't the dark browns that normally accompanied such deeper-colored features. I watched, trying to place the familiarity, until he moved into a position where the other person obscured my view.

My eyes stretched wide when beyond the two, a blue scaled tail stretched out. Another crooning sound pierced the night at the same time I placed the young man's resemblance—Imrythel. A hand seized my arm and pulled me around. I gasped, lost balance, and landed on my backside. Something I couldn't see pressed hard over my mouth. A hand?

My eyes roamed but found nothing. No one. In my ear, I felt a hot breath and heard muffled words. "Back to the room, lovely."

Kyr? I sucked in air through my nose and lifted my hand to call the wind.

Another force batted it down. And a second muffled voice commanded. "The room. Now." Then the force urged me upward. The force on my mouth gone, and another touch pulled me forward by the wrist.

"Misha?" I hissed.

"Hush," he answered.

I started, "Why can't—"

"Shhh." The invisible hands pushed me back into the dark room.

Sounds rustled toward the bed.

I swiveled my head until the Small Folk man appeared standing beside the rumpled bed.

"Wh-What are you doing here?" I stammered. "Where's Kyr? Why couldn't I see? How did you . . ."

But I lost my words as Kyr materialized beside her mate, lifting her hand away from a stone on the bed. My mouth worked wordlessly, disbelievingly. Misha dug in a small pouch and whispered a few seemingly foreign words as he placed another stone in my palm. They both picked up the ones they'd placed on the bed. Their forms shimmered, dimmed for a second, but they didn't vanish.

Misha said, "Okay, now we're ready."

I felt no different as I gaped at the tiny, nearly clear but dull stone.

"Invisibility spell," Kyr said and shooed her hands

toward me. "You're hidden too." She widened her eyes and put a finger over her lips in a shh motion, then added, "They'll dull sounds some, but not completely. Now, on with you, lovely."

"Hold on." At the door, I hesitated, curious about how the stones and spell worked and still itching to go toward the castle to help the dragon and find what I'd lost. "My scimitynes. They took them." If these stones allowed me to travel unseen throughout the castle, I desperately wanted to go in search of them. Returning both myself and my gifted weapons would be the best avoidance of Thalaj's impending scorn.

"No, no! This way." Kyr urged me along behind Misha.

He halted at the next corner with his hand holding us back as he searched the open space. As I crouched behind him, he pointed across the open space and slightly to the left. "That's the way back."

I grabbed his shoulder. "How long do we have until dawn? With these, we can go back, help the dragon, and get my weapons before we leave."

Misha gave me a sideways glance, impatient and warning.

Kyr grunted. "Nope. Not an option. We're to get you off this cloud." She nodded at Misha who turned and darted toward the escape. Kyr prodded me into a jog behind her mate. "Thalaj will take care of the rest."

"What?" I barked, stopping in the open. Thalaj was here? On the sky island? Taking care of . . . what?

Misha turned and scurried back to me. Exacerbated, he grabbed my wrist, and pulled. His words came harshly if hushed still. "We're getting you off this sky island, weapons or no. And that dragon is strong enough to care for herself."

But I'd forgotten the dragon when learning Thalaj had come too. Where was he now? I tried to resist but felt torn between my own safety and my first guard's. "If Thalaj is here, we should help and leave together. What if he gets hurt?" What I left unsaid broke me almost as much as the thought of his pain. My scimitynes were gifts from him and I didn't believe I could bear their loss.

Misha barked again, "He has a stone too." Then he grumbled, "Not that people can see that man moving in the night."

Kyr added, "You worry overmuch, lovely. He'll meet us back where you left Hoaris. Now we're under orders. We must move."

I went, driven by a niggling feeling that I should trust my companions as the last time I hadn't, I'd walked right into Alto-Trea's trap. We scurried across the remaining yard. My heart wrenched when another keening echoed from behind through the predawn skies. Misha turned back, grasped my hand, and pulled me along. With quick steps, we trotted down clouded stairs, our destination the roof of one of the crumbling buildings. There, I stopped and looked up. Watching us without movement, Filtch stood. His eyes settled directly upon me, apparently seeing through the spelled stones and holding my gaze. Still, even as I'd made an escape and his scheme would no longer unfold like he desired, he portrayed no emotion.

Something about the Cloud Courtier disguised as patron of the casteless held my attention while I asked Misha, "How did you know where to find me?"

"Thalaj came to us and we returned before you left. We followed you, then waited."

"Did you go inside the office while I spoke with

Filtch?"

"No, lovely. We didn't get the chance to slip into the room," answered Kyr.

"So we waited outside," Misha added.

"Why didn't you save me earlier while I was asleep in the bedroom?" My voice sounded distant even to my own ears and my eyes remained on the Cloud Courtier.

"We had to wait for you to wake up. We're not strong enough to carry you so far," Kyr whispered.

I tilted my head to Filtch. He mirrored my action, and I felt my brow grow heavy. "Misha, you know he sees us?"

"Impossible." Misha stood beside me and looked up. "But if he does, we're away now, and we need to get further."

I raised a hand. Filtch did the same. The young man from the Great Sands I'd seen before stepped up to his side and followed his gaze. But his look was entirely blank, unseeing, and confused. Filtch smiled, grabbed the man's arm, and turned him away. They retreated from the misty edge. Gone.

The hidden blue dragon wailed again—the sound sadder than any I could fathom. Misha and Kyr both flinched. I tensed, my eyes prickling. Hers would be another soul that rested heavily upon my heart. Mayhap another day we could save her too.

Misha shook his head. "I don't know how he could see us, but that's even more reason to move."

"No." If he could see us, he could see Thalaj. "I can't leave Thalaj."

Kyr pulled on my cloak. "Trust your protector. He has

sufficient training with the Unseen. He knows how to escape these situations."

"She's right, and Thalaj said as much," urged Misha.

I finally peeled my eyes away from the edge where Filtch had been and looked at the small man. Most of me wanted to pull back, run up the cloud stairs, and protect my first guard from any further harm on my behalf. Another part wanted to rescue the dragon from whatever her fate. Something seemed off about the people from the Great Sands and why they were present at a Cloud Castle on the coast of the Syrensea. But the other part of me— wiser part, I suspected—knew the Small Folk were right.

"Trust him," Misha implored.

With a final glance back, I decided.

And fled.

◇◇◇◇◇◇◇◇

ONCE AGAIN WITHIN THE run-down room where I'd spent the majority of the prior day, we found Hoaris leaning up against the wall, head thrown back, and mouth hanging wide open. A soft, rhythmic snore rumbled from his throat. The casteless—Gnat, Flea, and Honera—were no longer present, and it surprised me that Hoaris would sleep without a watch. I placed my invisibility stone on the table, and with that out of my hands, Misha and Kyr vanished. They uttered some quick words, and once done, they both stood visibly at the table as they dropped the stones into their pouches.

I thought how strange their magic was, not tied to a source within but to words and objects. They simply said some phrases in their strange language and things happened—unexpected things. For my magic to work, I needed a connection to the sky or a water source, and it always built from inside and resulted in wind or rain unless I pushed harder. With enough energy, I could gather the thunder and lightning, but those expressions of my sorcery were only possible because I manipulated the winds in the atmosphere to build energy. The other castes had similar focused magic—the Cloud Courtiers relied on a force inherent to Nantai earth to float their castles and change appearances, for example—but the Small Folk could learn certain ways with words and cause all sorts of things to happen. I wondered if others could learn their ways but put the thought aside and went to Hoaris to wake the burly man.

As I leaned down, Kyr hissed, "I wouldn't—"

But before her words sank in, Hoaris grabbed my wrist with lightning speed and had me pinned in a sitting position against the wall, his broad hand holding my throat. With a small squeeze, he could sever my airway. I latched one hand onto his forearm. A rush surged through my body and my heart pounded like wilderbeasts stampeding across the plains. With my other hand, I reached for the storm's power. A gust came rushing through the window, howling around the room, and recognition registered upon Hoaris's face. He released me and sagged at my side.

Kyr giggled. "Red Bear doesn't wake happily, lovely."

Hoaris scrubbed his hands over his face, rasping over his beard. "Did you . . ." He cleared his sleep deadened throat. "Did Filtch agree to send our message?"

"No," I said.

He looked at the Small Folk, confusion clearly drawing his brows to a peak. "So, what do we do now?"

Misha said, "We wait for your cold friend."

Thalaj.

I still worried but also wondered about Honera and the boys. "Where are the casteless?"

"Couple of dice games after you went, they left too." Hoaris lumbered to his feet, scrubbing sleep from the corners of his eyes. "Where is Thalaj anyway?"

At his question, a heavy clunk on the table echoed around the room. Thalaj stood, becoming visible as he left a spelled stone visible on the table. "I'm here."

I sucked in a breath, my hand covering my mouth. He appeared as he had before, carrying naught but his own weapons, but the angles on his face seemed chiseled in ice. By force, I had to hold myself in place to keep from leaping up, soaring toward him, and throwing my arms about him in a hug. Even if he hadn't reclaimed my scimitynes as I'd hoped, he'd returned safely before Alto-Trea's cloud castle departed. For that alone, I said thanks to the Holy Triad. Outside, morning was just beginning to break and Otarr would soon assume his watch over the day. If the Cloud Courtier's orders held true, the castle would be misting away like a morning fog. Standing, I approached him slowly, heeding the warning in his posture and still fighting the desire to rush to him. He stared at me, his dark eyes cold and his anger chilling the space between us. Frost Fighters controlled heat in the air, dispelling it at will as Thalaj often did when he was angry.

"I'm so sorry I wouldn't listen," I said. Clasping and wringing my fingers, I hoped his angst would ease now that we were all safely away. I refused to break eye contact as he glared at me, feeling I deserved his admonishment. So I waited.

He squeezed his eyes closed and took an audible

breath. As he exhaled, the air fogged. My face felt cold and the hairs on my arms rose, but as soon as the cold had arrived, it receded. When he opened his eyes, he'd regained control. I touched his arm, growing more hopeful when he didn't recoil.

Hoaris leaned heavily on the other end of the table. "So . . . this Filtch person didn't agree to deliver the message. Whadda we do now? How do we get the message to Sarangarel?"

Kyr chattered, "Who's Sarangarel?"

I sighed. "She's the gnoble of the Stone Singer caste residing in the city's keep at the moment. We had hoped she would sponsor a ship to sail across the Syrensea."

I crossed to the window, regretting to some extent that we'd followed Honera and hadn't made progress on understanding what it'd cost to hire a crew for ourselves. The one sailor had warned of his departure on the morn; had we missed an opportunity through our dalliance? Would a white-flagged ship still remain at the docks by the time we returned?

Misha folded his arms over his chest and issued a harrumph, pulling me from my musings.

"You people and your castes," he said.

Raising both brows, I stared at him wordlessly. The statement seemed odd after the story he'd told me of his exile. The small people had rankings too, so how was it that ours seemed so strange?

Chatter passed between Misha and Kyr, too fast for me to follow. Just as I was considering using the invisibility spelled stones myself, Misha said, "I'll go in. Where is this gnoble?"

"Wait." I looked intently at each of my friends' faces,

dreading the need to deliver the news I'd learned from Filtch. "I'm not sure she'll accept us now."

Thalaj quirked a brow. "What do you mean? Gaining an audience was the challenge. She'd certainly listen to a request from an Evangale."

I held a fist to my mouth, trapping the words that thought to spew forth, and considered how much I should share regarding my conversation with the Swan. I crossed the room and took a seat. At length, I said, "I fear I may have lost any influence I once possessed."

A chair scraped across the floor, and Thalaj dropped into the seat beside me. "At the risk of repeating myself, Mairynne, what do you mean?"

I took a deep breath and told them everything. That Karynne had ascended to the Serpentine Throne. That she'd offered a reward to have me and Thalaj returned to Stormskeep. That I didn't know how it all had happened. And that it would be risky now to trust any one of the gnobles at this point. My hand locked around my necklace stones, heat suffusing my palm. "But one thing is certain . . . we need to get out of Nantai, find my father, and then return to set things right in Stormskeep."

As I'd narrated the information from the night before, Hoaris, Misha, and Kyr had also taken seats, and we sat in silence for a long while after I finished.

Awkwardly, Misha asked, "Why don't we hunt down that Cloud Courtier and make him ferry us across the sea? He seemed fond of you as we left."

Shaking my head, I said, "That Cloud Courtier is as dangerous as they come, I believe. Filtch is an illusion, and I still don't know fully what he has to do with the casteless. His real name is Alto-Trea, and I wouldn't trust him with the simplest task, let alone something so important."

Thalaj agreed. "All that matters little, though. Their magic is connected to Nantai. Their sky islands wouldn't travel past the Vesterisles."

Hoaris stood and held out a hand to Misha. "Give me one of those invisibility rocks. I'll go in and find this Sarangarel."

My first guard placed a hand on the big man's arm, urging him back into his chair. "Hoaris, can you watch while I sleep for a couple of hours?"

"I should go now," he objected. "Catch her before the day gets too far in."

Thalaj shook his head. "If I can get a couple of hours of sleep, we can all go together. We'll find her while she's alone. She'll listen to us together"—his face hardened—"whether by her own will or by force, she'll listen."

ELEVEN

The Stone Lady

INVISIBLE BY THE SPELL on the stones and unable to speak lest we give ourselves away, the five of us snuck through the stone halls in search of the Stone Lady, Sarangarel, occasionally ducking to one side as a group of Stone Singer servants passed. The house was abuzz with daily activity, and if I were to guess, these people had the keenest sense of hearing of all the castes and the casteless. Though seemingly so graceless in their stout statures, their ears twitched at the slightest sound. When others were around, we carefully matched our steps to theirs lest we draw attention to our invisible intrusion.

After some time, we arrived at a room from where more Singers came and went than the others. Standing in a nearby corner, we watched and waited to discern the patterns of the servants. When a last group filtered out, Kyr scurried forth and held the door while we slid inside. The rooms to my measure were almost a replica of my own at Stormskeep, and I felt a momentary pang, a longing for home. But as I looked around at the things, the differences became starker than the similarities. The Stone craftsmen had inlaid gemstones upon everything—a mirror trimmed in shimmering green, a nearby sofa with burnt-umber stones on the woodwork, the utensils on the table decorated with white stones on the handles. The glittering stones gave the room an ostentatious feel similar to the necklace Sarangarel had presented at my ascension.

The rooms were quiet, and the five of us stood in silence for several moments trading questioning glances until the soft flap of a page turning alerted us to the space behind the curtains. Someone was reading on the veranda behind the material gently swaying in the breeze. I, being the closest to the door, went through and found Lady Sarangarel reclined in a chair and indeed reading a book.

The vision before me stole my breath. No longer in regalia fit for ascension pomp, the curves I'd judged before as stocky and stout now appeared plump and inviting. Her hair, customarily woven in tight braids before, now hung in a heavy dark-brown curtain over one shoulder in flowing waves. Her slanted eyes caressed the words on the page, and I wondered how they might caress a person.

Heat suffused my cheeks as Thalaj stepped to my side, nudging me to behind her.

As we'd decided before, he would present himself to her alone and beg her help in their situation. We held no certainty our plan would work, but it seemed worth a try. Mayhap I allowed him this action out of guilt over my previous poor decision or possibly wisdom lay in deferring to his greater experience.

Thalaj placed the stone upon the railing, whispered the words, and lifted his hand. The air shimmered around him as the spell lifted and he became visible to more than just our party. I twisted my lips, musing that he could speak the spell while I still needed assistance from the Small Folk. Something I'd need to revisit.

Sarangarel didn't move, didn't so much as lift her head from the words upon the pages of her book, and her voice was even as she spoke. "Have you orders for my death, Shadow?"

Thalaj gave a wry smile, one that said many things but nothing at all, one that would tell you things true and imagined; but having not peered up from her book, Sarangarel could not have seen this smile. I, on the other hand, watched as he stalked in front of her like the predatory nekodai of the Iced Plains. Grace and power coiled within every one of his muscles. He prowled. Death walking the veranda in the daylight and preparing himself for a civilized conversation.

Sarangarel moved her hand to the table at her side, lifting a steaming cup to her lips. She sipped but still said naught. Had I been the one faced with such an intruder, I don't believe I would have been as calm as this gnoble. Either she had made peace with whatever fate and Thalaj had in store for her, or she knew something we did not. I looked toward the door, but seeing no other threat, turned back to the scene.

Thalaj tempered his smile and said, "Quite the contrary, Lady Sarangarel. I have come to ask your help."

The thought might have startled someone less poised than the Stone Lady, but from my point of view, she didn't move so much as her little finger. Things between the two seemed tensely cordial, but Thalaj's posture said anything but.

"Thalaj Northerngale, First Guard to Kōgō Mairynne Evangale," she said, my name a bit louder than the rest.

Folding the book and placing it onto the table, she added, "The rumors of your stealth are true, but I must inquire about this stone you use." Her head tilted slightly, suggesting she appraised the stone as she finished.

"This?" Thalaj reached for the stone. "It's merely a rock." Having dispelled the magic when he placed it on the railing, he tossed the thing to her.

Sarangarel raised her hand slowly as if she had all the time under Otarr's watchful gaze, and even so slow, she plucked the stone from midflight. "Then I must inquire after how it sings of invisibility."

"That is beyond my knowledge," Thalaj said simply with a small shrug. It wasn't a lie. Though he could use the words to activate and deactivate the spell, I didn't believe he had the casting knowledge to bespell stones. At least it was a talent I'd never witnessed.

Misha and Kyr were smiling beside me, but they stifled their chatter for the time being in favor of maintaining the silence. Hoaris stood stock-still, hand on his hilt, and ready for whatever might come next, but he betrayed no reaction to the conversation before us.

Lady Sarangarel twirled the plain white stone in front of her face, examining something I couldn't discern. "This is no natural song," she mused. "The veins remain quiet." And with that, she tossed it back.

Thalaj's movement, unlike hers, was quick. His hand blurred as he snatched the stone from the air.

She tilted her head slightly. "I'll leave you your secret for now. But I do find it strange that you, of all the people in Nantai, would be here begging a favor given the fact that there is a price posted for you that would make it well worth my while to detain you. But I am no foolish woman. Please"—she flourished a hand—"be on with it."

Thalaj tipped his head forward respectfully. "Lady Sarangarel, we would ask for you to arrange passage for our party of five upon a ship across the Syrensea."

The gnoble of the Stone Singers barked a throaty laugh. "I have two questions for you, Shadow. First, why is it you assume this is within my powers? Secondly, what would be in this bargain for me or my people?"

The way they used titles and names seemed a dance. They traded them as if they would either honor or slight the other. I couldn't distinguish the intentions. *Shadow* would seem, in my mind and the gnoble's tone, to be an insult, but the title meant prestige to those of the Unseen. Would Sarangarel possess such knowledge? By the grace of the Triad, though, she hadn't referred to his blended heritage, both Storm Sorcerer and Frost Fighter. Perhaps there was a tinge of respect laced into her words, but it confounded me.

I rubbed the bespelled stone still resting in my hand and hiding me from sight. A quick toss would reveal my presence and allow me to join the banter, but a watchful Hoaris read my intent and shook his head slowly. He was right. Prudence bade that I should trust and wait for Thalaj's cue as to when I could safely join the conversation.

My first guard rubbed a hand over his stubbled jawline. "I am unable to make an offer we can pay in the present hour, but I do speak on behalf of the Evangales."

Sarangarel stood, issuing another humorless laugh. "*The* Evangale *herself* placed the reward upon your return to Stormskeep. Why am I to believe that you would be able to offer more?" She sauntered toward Thalaj, swaying a hip suggestively toward him. I felt a stab through my chest, and my mouth went bone-dry. She ran a finger, nails lacquered blood red, down his chest. Her eyes followed.

I made to move, but Hoaris held up a forestalling hand.

Thalaj glanced over her head to where I stood. He couldn't see my reaction without being under the cloak of invisibility, and for that small wonder, I felt immense relief. Jealousy was an unbecoming mask upon any who wore it.

Sarangarel lifted her gaze back to his. "And, were I to detain you, mightn't the youngest Evangale come in search of her most favored guard?"

I took one step. Hoaris gave me a look, his lips in a tight line, eyes wide and hard with warning. On a slow inhale, I worked to hold myself in place, releasing the air bit by bit.

Thalaj smiled, but I saw naught but calculation in his dark eyes. "There isn't need for you to wait." He lifted a hand in my general direction. His eyes followed but looked to my side ever so slightly. Naturally, as eye contact with the invisible was nigh impossible.

Unless the person in question was Alto-Trea.

I shook away that thought. Another time.

The Stone Singer turned. Shorter than me, as I could tell by the top of her head not quite reaching Thalaj's shoulder. Indeed, she was lovely. She wore her dark curls as a waist-length cloak, and her plentiful curves— shadowlike under the simple shift and so unlike my own—begged for a caress. Swallowing and thoroughly confused, I stood straighter and reminded myself that despite whatever my sister had done that I was still the rightful heir to the Serpentine Throne by Tennō Atheryn

Evangale's decree. That was if, and a doubtful if, my father *had* perished.

With the thoughts of Father, the stone resting beneath my tunic flared, reassuring me further.

Hoaris held out a hand for my stone. I can only imagine the vision Sarangarel beheld as I shimmered into view. Each time I'd seen someone revealed, I'd also seen the stone they'd dropped. Handing my stone to someone who remained unseen, it must have appeared that I stepped from thin air. I pushed my chin a little higher, the thought giving me more confidence. And there upon the balcony in the open air, I spread my other hand and called the wind.

A soft breeze lifted my hair and stirred Sarangarel's hair-made cloak. Behind her, Thalaj gave a small smile as our eyes met. Then he said, "It is our understanding that your caste always welcomes new opportunities for trade and the possibility of discovering gemstones currently unavailable in Nantai."

"And so," I added, the imagined bonds upon my voice finally releasing, "given your relative wealth, we hoped that you would sponsor a ship on our behalf. Once we've completed our travels and I return to Stormskeep, I will ensure that the treasurers send thrice the bounty upon our souls."

"Indeed, that is quite the offer, young kōgō."

I looked at her curiously, still confounded by the usage of the titles, and even more so by this one. Across all castes, that was the most sacred title for the empress of the people, and she had just given it to me. Yet my sister had ascended to the Serpentine Throne. Did that mean Sarangarel supported my plight rather than Karynne's? Did that mean she knew more than she let on? Did that mean she would help? Instead of asking these questions directly, I waited to see how she would play her turn.

She began to pace, though to call it pacing would give it urgency. No, she began walking, swinging her hips with every step, back and forth along the edge of the veranda, and in silence.

I waited.

Observe and listen.

And Thalaj waited as well.

At length, she started calculations aloud. She named off the crew members necessary to man a ship, each with a number attached. How she kept the figures within her head I couldn't fathom, but I had never been one for numbers.

"How long do you believe this journey will take?" she asked.

I had no answer.

Thalaj, clearly unable to guess at a duration either, said, "As long as it must."

"And to where did you say you wished to sail?"

I took a breath to speak, but my guard held up a hand. "We didn't. Only across the Syrensea."

Sarangarel sighed. "You must forgive me, but without these details, I fail to see how this voyage is worth my time and investment."

Urgency built and fueled my angst over the possibility of losing the opportunity. I started, "Lady Saranga—" but she silenced me with a small, dismissive wave.

"Kōgō and her Shadow," Sarangarel mused, tapping a lacquer-tipped finger against her lips. She walked the terrace for several more long moments in silence. Clearly more variables and the sky's gods only knew what other thoughts raced through her mind, but she reserved those reflections.

I went to stand beside Thalaj. Cold poured off of him in waves, a sure sign that he worked with all his might to maintain solid control. Though he managed them well enough, politics and negotiations were not his favored activities. I understood. And like him, I felt better, more at ease, with a blade in each hand and performing the dances of death. I'd only begun to learn, but he'd honed them for so many years, they existed in all his movements. This I knew now as his student. But there on Lady Sarangarel's veranda was not a place for such things, and then was not the time. He understood that as well as I. After our conversations with the deck hands on the docks, after my encounter with Filch, and with the measly mon within our purses, the Stone Lady seemed our last hope for gaining this passage. All we needed now was for her to decide in our favor.

Sarangarel shook her head. "My people have a saying. Mayhap you're familiar with it?" She stopped, facing us and awaiting our answer.

Thalaj and I exchanged a clueless look.

"Well. It goes like so . . . 'The world's heart gem holds the steepest value, albeit a single stone and one nigh impossible to obtain. Shallow stones will provide.' "

The last of this I'd heard from her lips before. She'd said as much upon the sky island that boasted the High Cloud Court during one of the many ascension ceremonies I'd endured. Court. Having the first part of the saying, I understood better, and it made sense to the nature of the Stone Singers. They were a solid people, and though the gems they traded were of great value to their patrons in

Nantai and beyond, they only dug deep enough to provide for their people.

Her eyes were rueful, couldn't quite make contact with either my own or Thalaj's. But then she changed in an instant. "But I am well provided for and have more than necessary. My people have done well under Tennō Atheryn Evangale, then under Kōgō Mairynne Evangale." She looked at me then. "Although the short time you ruled may not warrant entries in the history books. There are signs that the newest leader of the Nantai people has less pure intentions in her heart."

Karynne.

The thought sliced into me, a painful knife searing me in two. I despised that my eldest sister sowed discord among my people. I'd worried at one time when she'd been so eager to guide my decisions, but during my ascension I'd believed those issues resolved. How naïve I had been. Thalaj moved closer; had he sensed my pain? Nadia, my mother's twin sister, had been the one person I had felt most confident would hold to my father's ideals and to mine. Regretfully, it seemed she no longer held such power.

Someday, somehow, I had to rectify the situation in Stormskeep as well . . . *after* I found Father.

The stones flared.

"Your sentiment is much welcome, Sarangarel," I said in gratitude.

Sarangarel lifted her chin. "There is naught for you to welcome. I believe our people need you as kōgō. I believe your father showed wisdom in his choice of heir. I do not know how your sister came into her ascension or what happened to Nadialynne Riversgale." Her eyes darkened. "I do hope your sweet aunt is well," she added with a mournful glance.

I took a step closer. "Does this mean you will help us?"

She pursed her lips. "I will, but as you well know, bargains with the Stone Singers are ne'er inexpensive." Her eyes shifted between me and Thalaj.

"Then name your price, Lady Sarangarel," Thalaj snapped.

Chills ran over my arms. I could hear ice in his voice. His tolerance for such politics ran thin, and I breathed a sigh of relief that we hadn't allowed him to come into this meeting alone. In truth, he should have dealt with Filtch while I managed the Stone Lady. I glanced over to the space where Hoaris and the Small Folk had been standing—still stood, I hoped. I considered the Tsinti and our time with them, the people in Safaia and Kōkai, even the sailor Jerek; all people in Nantai deserved better.

Whatever her conditions, I would honor them.

"I have three requirements," she said, her eyes flashing deviously. She stepped to the railing where Thalaj had deposited his stone. "First, you will share with me the secret of your unnatural stone."

Thalaj shifted, moving slightly in front of me. "That is easy enough," he said, "but we will have your remaining demands before we decide."

"Of course, I will send a party of my people on the journey with you. They shall be allowed to pursue errands on my behalf." Sarangarel looked past my guard, holding and embracing my eyes with her own. "And finally, I will have Mairynne for the evening—for the late meal *and* to warm my bed this night."

TWELVE

The Yisun

BRIGHT OTARR DIMMED AND made his way toward
sleep for the evening, and I stood within the Stone Lady's
suite, unable to divine where the night would take us.
Offering her the secret of the spelled stones and agreeing
to take her people with us upon the journey had been the
easy part of the deal. For the rest . . . the negotiation took
the better part of the day.

As soon as she'd made her demand, the heat had
dissipated from the veranda. Shards of ice had flashed
blue in my guard's eyes, and I'd believed only violence
would resolve the situation. As stunned as I had been
by Sarangarel's demand, I had stammered to object. But
Thalaj's outcry had overshadowed my own. And despite
invisibility, Hoaris's blade had sung free of its scabbard,
calling Sarangarel's attention to the seemingly empty
space near the door. I had reached for my first guard,
seized his arm just before he started for the Stone Lady.

"There is little cause for attack. It's merely a decision
to be made," I whispered. "*My* decision." Earlier, she

had been so unwilling to even consider our plight for any reasons beyond her own wealth. That she asked so little else as payment made her offer near impossible to refuse.

When he'd turned to me, his face had been a whitish shade of green. His dark eyes had implored with me. "Mairynne, no. You cannot."

Afterward, my attention had been focused for hours upon trying to convince him that this would be okay. I'd stopped short of issuing a command. After much debate, and once provided with comfortable accommodations just across the hall from Sarangarel's rooms, he had relented. But he'd carried a bitterness with him that made my heart ache.

Within the first quiet moments while Sarangarel went to speak with a servant about our meal, I had a long overdue opportunity to sort out my own feelings about the arrangement. My mind. My heart. My body. They were all at odds with one another like three siblings vying desperately to have a parent's sole attention for herself—even if only for a time. That scenario, I knew well; but to have that same battle raging within myself was a matter unto itself. Though my mind spun with all of my first guard's logical arguments—that I was selling my body, that we would figure out another way, that I was too young yet to understand the implications—my heart ached for the words he hadn't said. Throughout this confusion, my body tingled with anticipation. I had noticed her voluptuous beauty early in our meeting, and I had felt a pang of jealousy that she'd swayed her curves in Thalaj's direction. Whether the jealousy had been over him or her, I couldn't be certain.

And for all of the desire building, Thalaj was right. Indeed, I was inexperienced when it came to this— beyond the years where other girls had explored such things, young nevertheless.

But as the princess and the decreed heir, I hadn't the liberties of most. Once, I'd listened dreamily as Jessamyne Feathergale had spoken of her first kiss. We'd giggled over her description of the awkward wetness, but I'd imagined it as my own experience with the young man by the name of Northerngale who'd recently joined the guard that protected the royal family.

Thalaj.

I sighed.

Upon that thought, Sarangarel appeared with two fluted glasses, a deep amber liquid within. She'd changed clothes, now wearing a strapless shift the color of the deep red stones that decorated her neck and wrists. The dress shimmered as it caught Otarr's dying light. She handed me a glass and placed her own on a table upon which I assumed we'd dine. From a small cabinet, she retrieved more gemstones, each roughly the size of her fist. As she placed them upon the table, she closed her eyes briefly. When she lifted her hand, they began to glow.

She smiled, more beautiful than she'd been in the daylight, and lifted her own glass to me in a toast. "The wine will ease you, my kōgō." To my ears, her voice sounded at once a soft and warm caress around the title I hadn't wanted before. There and then, I found her use of it more inviting than threatening. Despite the knowledge that she'd purchased me for the night, I craved what she offered—whatever that was.

I wondered briefly how this would impact my ties with Thalaj, but I put that thought out of my mind. Though I would have welcomed more, our relationship hadn't been one of intimacy. He'd countered that notion by repeatedly citing the impurity of his bloodlines. Another idea I cared little about. But this evening, he had no place within Sarangarel's rooms. Dinner went on, light conversation ensued, and I took my second glass of wine; my soul eased while Selene climbed into the sky above Kōkai.

The meal complete, Sarangarel took my hand and led me into her bedchamber. I stopped at the door, pulling my hand from hers. What terror she read written across my face, I couldn't say. Yet her only reaction was a small smile. Circling the room, she touched several stones, singing them to life and casting the room in a soft amber light.

When she returned to me, she offered a soft shift. "Here, you'll be more comfortable for the evening in this rather than those travel clothes. I'll be back shortly." And she left me alone in the most private of her rooms.

Examining the material of the shift she had offered, it glittered, and I looked closer. The seamstress had woven a thousand or more tiny white gems into the fabric. I marveled at the softness given that stones decorated it. As I placed my own clothes on a chair nearby, the bronze cuff a garnish on top, words from earlier rang through my mind: "... purchased . . . a whore . . ." The Nantai people didn't frown upon the profession. In truth, in Tsanseri's court, the Courtiers and those who visited celebrated it. The only people who would ever know of this assignation were those within my small party, and beyond that knowledge, only Sarangarel and I would know what transpired within these rooms. With eyes closed, I took a deep, cleansing breath and let it out on an audible sigh.

"Mairynne"—Sarangarel's voice hugged my name as it had my title—"you need not worry or fear. I will not force you into any act against your wishes." When she finished, her voice was near, behind me.

She'd read my worries well, but where there was

trepidation, there was also desire. I turned with a smile and reached nervously for her. "May Atun, Otarr, and Selene help me," I said, looking deep into her eyes and moving my body closer to hers. "Lady Sarangarel, my body has an appetite I've never truly known. Show me if you will, not because I am offering myself as payment, but because you have the same desire as I. If this is anything less than that, I ask that we not dive further into this intimacy."

She licked her lips. "It is naught but desire, my kōgō." She cupped my cheek and our lips met.

So much tenderness.

Anything but awkward, she tasted sweet and rich like the wine. For many hours into that night, we explored one another, sought pleasure, laughed, and within each other's arms, we erased another line between our castes.

⬦⬦⬦⬦⬦⬦

I AWOKE TO A new and colorful world, my body and soul having experienced delights I hadn't imagined possible. My muscles felt strained in new and unexpected places. Within the drapery around Lady Sarangarel's bed, cocooned in fluffy blankets and plump pillows, she kissed me awake from my neck up to my lips. A smile spread across my face when I looked up into her eyes.

She returned the smile and thanked me for an amazing evening, but then regret settled over her brow. "While I'd relish spending another day here with you, I have duties. We should make the arrangements for your ship."

"Wait." I reached for her, ducked my head for a moment in shyness, and then lifted my gaze again. "I must thank you too for last night." My voice wavered, but it was all the grace I could muster.

She squeezed my hand and pulled me from the bed. We both stood naked and glorious in Otarr's morning light.

"Would you bathe before we deal with your jealous young man?" Her smile seemed downright devious.

"He . . . he's not *mine*," I stammered, blinking in disbelief.

She flashed a knowing smile and said, "More yours than you know," as she reached for a bathing cloth from a tall set of drawers. "Despite the privilege you have granted me for a night, I won't have you beyond. You'll have him and he'll have you for much longer."

The words reminded me of those the Zofi had said when we'd first encountered Thalaj working within his bonds. *"That one,"* the Tsinti witch wife had said, *"he will always be there for you. There will come a time when you'll doubt but rest easy as he will always return."* I hoped they held true.

I bathed for the first time since the caverns beneath the trading town, Safaia, luxuriating in the sweetly scented waters. The feeling of cleanliness gave me a sudden flush of embarrassment over the intimacy with Sarangarel and having not washed before, but she hadn't protested. I emerged into Sarangarel's empty main room with hair wet and wearing the freshest of my travel clothes. It felt as if I were a new person. Despite the pleasure of the night before and the new appetites awoken within me, my journey called.

I grasped the stones at my neck. "Father," I said on a sigh.

Heat flared to life in my palm, but it seemed slower to warm this time. Somewhere he awaited, and time grew critical. I'd reset my determination and stepped toward the door, intent on finding my travel companions. We'd dallied here in the City by the Sea for far too long.

Sarangarel reappeared as I reached the door and exited her rooms first. Across the hall, she knocked and waited. It was Misha who answered and welcomed us inside. He and the Stone Lady bantered for a bit while I searched the rooms, finding only Kyr and Hoaris, both wide-eyed and brows raised with apparent worry, or mayhap warning. Where was Thalaj? Did I dare ask?

But the conversation between Sarangarel and Misha persisted, filling the room. At length, Sarangarel asked, "Now that I've returned her, will you teach me how to place the spell upon your stones?"

Misha's laugh rang like chimes in the wind. "I cannot teach you such a spell. Your mouth isn't formed properly to make the words."

She stiffened. "But this is part of the bargain."

Kyr jumped in. "The bargain was"—she raised both brows, widening her eyes—"'you will share with me the secret of your unnatural stone.' The secret is that there is a spell cast upon the rock by the Small Folk. There is a word, mekoilieu, that you speak to activate and deactivate the spell. That word is pronounceable in your tongue, and therefore you may use the spells already cast upon the stone. You made no demands that we teach you how to create the spell." Kyr shrugged and gave me a wink.

I mouthed the word, committing it to memory, "Mekoilieu."

The Small Folk, if I had ever met any linguists, were the sheer embodiment. They'd caught me once or twice in the technicalities of my words and the nuances of language. Sarangarel looked at me as if she wanted to ask how I tolerated such insolence. All I could do was shrug in the same manner Kyr had done. But I didn't wink, because I knew too well her frustration.

Sarangarel lifted her chin, the paths in her mind working again. "Well and so. Does it have to be a particular stone, or will any gem work?"

Misha took a seat. "The only requirement is that it be of a solid color. Mottling within the rock won't hold that spell."

The Stone Lady went to another chest and pulled a handful of bright gems—greens, oranges, yellows, in various sizes but all small enough to tuck safely into one's pocket without being seen—and dumped them upon the table. Misha picked through them, found the three largest, and said, "Three. I will offer three. The spell wears on me, you see."

"And what of her?" Sarangarel pointed to Kyr.

They chattered, pitch too high and fast for my understanding, but at last, Kyr shook her head. "Our women aren't the spellcasters."

Misha added, "Things could go too awry. It's too much risk for her to try. I have offered more than you bargained for yesterday upon your balcony." He sat back from the stones, folding his arms over his chest, and allowed his dangling foot to swing some ways above the floor.

Sarangarel agreed, but within the set of her jaw, she betrayed that it displeased her to have her expectations lowered so.

"Find your young guard," she said to me, caressing my arm and grasping onto my hand. "I will retrieve the Singers who will accompany you over the Syrensea and return shortly." She rushed from the room, her hips swaying faster.

Hoaris barked a laugh. "You got her well, little one."

Misha gathered the small stones she'd left on the table—all except the three largest he'd set aside—and tucked them in his pouch.

I shot him a questioning stare.

He lifted a shoulder. "She left it up to us how exactly we shared that information. She should be more precise in her demands."

Hoaris roared again as Misha turned toward the three stones and began whispering over them.

"Where is Thalaj?" I asked, at last having the opportunity to satisfy my curiosity.

Hoaris turned solemn and pointed toward a door.

Kyr eyed me. "Careful, lovely."

Heedless of the warning in the big man's posture or upon the little woman's face, I went for the door. Inside, the moisture from my breath created clouds, and I rubbed my arms to create my own heat. He had drawn the curtains against Otarr's watchfulness. As the door behind me closed, the only light was a small slit in the heavy drapes. There wasn't enough to see the room given I'd entered from a brighter area. If it was a mirror layout of Sarangarel's, a bed lay to my left. I turned in that direction, but his word came from my other side.

"Here." Quiet and hoarse and gruff, a tone I had never heard in Thalaj's voice before.

I swallowed, thankful for the cover of darkness to hide the unspoken words I'm sure shone upon my face. "All is well. We should be able to set sail at first light. Lady Sarangarel has sent word to the docks and went to collect the party that will travel with us upon the ship."

"All. Is. Well?" he rasped. "More apt to say all is done." A surge of cold rolled from the direction of his voice.

I didn't know how to answer the short and bitter words, so I stood awkwardly wringing my hands until he spoke again.

"Leave me. I will come momentarily."

I went, the doorknob like ice under my touch. Time. Would time ease his cold rage? I'd give him that for now, but once we were on our way, I'd have to force conversation.

In the common area, I wondered if what Sarangarel had said was true. Could he possibly still be *my* young man, or had that changed after my choice last night? I remained torn, confused. He'd always told me that *we* couldn't be because of his blended blood. Was he angered because I'd chosen someone of an even lower caste or because he wanted something for us? He couldn't believe that I'd remain virginal for the entirety of my days, so it must have been that I'd chosen someone beneath me . . . and beneath even his station. The thought that he held so much stock in this hells-imposed caste hierarchy saddened me even more than that he'd rejected me under the claim of his unworthiness.

I dropped into the chair beside Kyr. She grabbed my wrist and squeezed, and when I looked up, she offered me deep sympathy in her eyes and a rueful smile.

Misha had finished spelling the stones and rested with his head against the back of the chair and his eyes closed.

Hoaris came over and placed a strong hand upon my shoulder. "Give him space, and he'll return."

The door slammed and heavy booted feet traipsed

inside—three Stone Singer men and two women stood to the side while Sarangarel walked between them, head held high and a bejeweled headdress closely resembling a crown resting upon a nest of sable-brown curls. She'd put away her soft and sheer robes for the regalia that bespoke gnobleship among her people. Her gait wasn't one of grace as she entered, but one of sturdiness and strength. Beyond doubt, I knew that she had earned her place among the Stone Stingers with that very prowess.

As I stood and rounded the table, she cut her eyes to me for only a split second, then held a hand toward the closest in an official manner. "These men will accompany you."

The two females boasted tight curls and plentiful breasts, but elsewise might have been men themselves for all I could tell under the heavy armor. Both men and women were broad at the shoulders. For the men, conversely, their chests lacked the soft round cleavage I'd so pleasantly experienced with Sarangarel the night before. Noting that she mentioned only men, I wondered if she intended the five of them to accompany my party or only the three males.

Sarangarel continued, "They are *yisun*." And she introduced them each in turn—Yisun Timur, Yisu Jaliqai, Yisun Nachin, Yisun Baidu, and Yisu Chambui.

I'd listened carefully, but with the foreign nature of the names and her natural inflection, even the first one mentioned escaped my mind.

The man, clearly reading my failure to retain the information, stepped forward with a cocked grin and a fist over his chest. "Timur. Yisun leader." Head bowed, he dropped to a knee briefly, then stood and returned to ranks.

I felt a cool draft from the side. Thalaj, hearing the commotion, must have decided to join us. A sigh lightened the weight in my shoulders, a grateful feeling that the breeze no longer resembled winter's gale.

The remaining Stone Singers made the same introductions as Timur, and I inferred that the first part—yisun, yisu for the women—was a title or shared name. A unit maybe. I'd ask later, but for the moment, I focused on their unique names. Timur, Jaliqai, Nachin, Baidu, Chambui; I worked to commit them to memory.

After we'd exchanged introductions, Sarangarel came to me and offered me a warm embrace. When we parted, she glanced at the door where I knew Thalaj stood, from where I still felt a cool breeze wafting around the room. Her eyes returned to mine, and she said quietly, "Thank you again, Kōgō. We'll certainly meet again." Then louder so the rest of the room could hear, "You must pardon me now. We have made all the arrangements with a ship called the *Swell Mistress*. You have the freedom to wander the house. Our servants will see to your meals here in this suite. You may rest in the rooms here this evening. Timur and the other yisun will return for you an hour before Selene passes the skies to Otarr. They will escort you to the docks where Captain Asahi will be ready for departure. I wish you well on your voyage." She kissed my cheek and left, followed by her yisun.

Alone with my small party, silence hung, a deadly chill in the room. I turned to meet dark and hard eyes and pleaded with my own gaze for him to thaw, if only a bit. Instead, he looked at no one other than me, then dropped his eyes to the floor. Without a word, Thalaj followed in the trail of Sarangarel and the yisun.

THIRTEEN

An Unexpected Gift

EARLY MORN—MORE THE SLEEPING hour than when people greeted the day in earnest—we awoke and departed from the keep at Kōkai. For the remainder of the day, into the eve, and during the night before we took our leave, I never encountered the Stone Lady again to bid her farewell. Though Sarangarel held a piece of my heart, the road, the sea, and Father called to me. And alas, farewells were too final. A smile lifted the corners of my lips as I looked over my shoulder at the white stone walls. One day, mayhap we would meet again.

On this night, the clouds hid Selene's face within the skies. Heavy and woolen, a gray cloak covered Kōkai, though there was no storm, no energy crackling, no thunder rolling or lightning biting through the darkness. It misted. I lifted my face toward the skies and tiny droplets prickled my nose, cheeks. The veil covering the City by the Sea, Nantai, and at least part of the Syrensea cried upon us.

Thalaj walked ahead. For my part, a distance between

us had grown I wouldn't have wished. Yet I could not change my decision to remain with Lady Sarangarel two nights before. And had I the magic of reversing time, I wouldn't choose differently. The only hope I had for him now was for time to heal the burden.

A door within my life's house had closed, another ending felt keenly as we approached the docks. Did the feeling lie in parting from Nantai? Or mayhap it was my soul ripping away from who and what I'd always known, away from all I considered my own. Certainly away from Thalaj. I peered back at the white-walled city, bidding her farewell. Time, distance, and the unknown awaited. The waves beyond the dock rolled gently, calling me onward. The last to go, I lowered my head and boarded the ship—a swell mistress indeed.

Captain Asahi shouted orders all around, sailors bustled about on his command, and my travel companions went below deck to settle into their cabins. The sailors loosened the ropes, freeing the vessel from the dock, and pushed away. The ship floated, directionless.

For all the commotion about me, I felt alone. We'd made it one step closer to finding Father, and the stones upon my breast verily vibrated their approval. Hot and cold surged against my skin.

Alas, I turned my back, making for the underbelly to settle into my cabin as well.

A screech pierced the night.

Whirling, I sucked in a breath. My body trembled.

The blue dragon snaked toward the *Swell Mistress* from the skies above. Sailors clamored away. In her claws, something dangled. As she arrived, she encircled the ship, slithering through the air above the deck. Her motion caused a gust. My hair whipped like a banner in the night.

On her third pass, she swooped down and dropped the package not a dozen paces from where I stood speechless.

She splashed into the water and raised her head above, fixating me with her diamond-like eye. Mayhap I imagined as much, but I believe she nodded just before she arose into the sky and disappeared into the blanket over Nantai.

I took one step . . . two . . .

The showers came heavier. My cloak clung damply to me as the water soaked through. My feet slipped on the wet deck as I rushed over. Pain sparked in my knees when I landed on the deck with a thud. Wet and reaching, I grappled at the straps.

Tears fell.

I grasped my weapon belt . . . the scimitynes Thalaj had bestowed upon me before we left Arashi. I clutched the scabbards to my chest . . . the very ones I'd believed lost forever to Alto-Trea upon his cloudy island.

Restored.

Thank you for reading

Call of the Syrensea

The Serpentine Throne Book Two

Other books in the series

Call of the Storm Sorcerer; April 19, 2021

Call of the Ryū Dragon; June 21, 2021

Call of the Scorched Empire; July 19, 2021

Call of the Maelstrom; August 23, 2021

For a free legend from The Serpentine Throne world, news on upcoming releases, promotions, and more, sign up for my newsletter here:

https://bit.ly/susanstradiottosnewsletter

OR

If you'd like to be a part of my street team to preview and review my books when they launch, sign up here:

https://bit.ly/SusansStreetTeam

OR

Continue reading for the first chapter of

Call of the Ryū Dragon

The Serpentine Throne Book Three

ONE

A Different Tack

HEAVY RAIN POUNDED THE decks of the *Swell Mistress*. Alone amidst the scurrying sailors, I stood once again with my weapon belt in hand and turned to watch our departure from Kōkai, more commonly called the City by the Sea, on the western coast of Nantai. The clouds overhead drifted northward, the downpour cleared, and my tears dried along with it. Otarr, the god who watches Nantai by day, broke over the horizon. The ship's nose pointed westward, and I moved to the back railing. The white-walled City by the Sea shrank as Otarr climbed into the skies. As we sailed west, away from my country, the blue dragon had returned my weapons—scimitynes given to me by my protector, Thalaj. And even though he had still not spoken to me after my assignation with Sarangarel, having the blades within my grasp brought hope.

Despite being estranged, I would offer Thalaj his space and maintain that nugget of hope within my heart.

Misty wind pelted my face, lifted my hair and made it

dance like a flag in the wind.

Captain Asahi took a space beside me, filled it with overwhelming height and lanky limbs. In my periphery, he swiped a cloth over his face, then secured his hat, the wide brim sheltering his eyes from the bright morning light. He leaned over and rested both elbows on the rail, which diminished him to roughly eye level. He trained his gaze to follow my own. "The Bright City we call her from the sea. A beauty, eh?"

"Yes." I gave him a weak smile. "It is."

Though hope shimmered within my heart because of the blue dragon's gesture, there were many things troubling me still. That morn, I sailed away from the only land I'd ever known and loved, and I had left Nantai in turmoil at the hands of my sister. Thalaj had distanced himself from me, still present in body but absent otherwise. And I toiled over Father, although the last should be a happier thought as we were yet another step closer.

"We normally don't move away from shore quite this fast." Asahi rocked back onto his heels, pulling me from my thoughts. Then he leaned forward again.

I turned to him, pursing my brows in wonder as to what he meant.

He chewed on a stick, brown and long, and shrugged. "That is to say, if you maintain this gale, we'll overshoot the Vesterisles by a league. I need to gather the remainder of my crew from Lu Galen, or *you* will be forced to man the sails."

Whatever he insinuated fell short of my understanding. The look on my face must have said as much.

He went on, "I'd ask you to keep your winds to a

minimum so I can keep control of this wench." He patted the boat railing thrice, winked, and left me there alone.

Pinching my eyes tight, I inhaled, collecting as much breath into myself as possible before releasing it. Of course. I'd called upon the wind without so much as a conscious thought. That he'd approached me about it meant the sailors must have been fighting against the force. I focused, brought the unconscious thoughts to the forefront of my mind, and released my hold on the magic. The wind eased. Mist no longer fell upon my cheeks, which glowed hot as I looked around. Watchful eyes averted here and there.

Facing the sunrise again, I decided I couldn't care or worry how others read my angst. How they judged me mattered little.

Before long, I felt another presence at my side—no, two. I stood between the two voluptuous yisu women. Unfortunately, they looked so much alike, I struggled to place which name belonged to which.

"The journey we face is long," the one on my right said.

I knew as much and fretted that it had begun at odds with the one person I trusted most in the world. With these two strangers, I hesitated to share the depth of my concern.

The woman on my right added, "You needn't worry overmuch." She sighed dismissively. "It's hard for men to brood for long."

"You're too blunt, Jaliqai," the other snapped. "I must apologize, my kōgō."

It eased me a bit that Jaliqai had been so forward. I chuckled. "Well and so, Chambui. I have enough confusion in my life. I appreciate Jaliqai's direct words. We'll all be better friends if you feel you may be forthright with me. And please, do not refer to me as kōgō."

"See, Chambui, she's who I said," Jaliqai said with an air of superiority.

To me, Chambui said, "Yisu Jaliqai may speak truth. Your shadowy friend will ease upon this ship because he has nowhere to run or hide from you." She glared at her friend. "But it could have been put to you with more delicacy and respect."

Jaliqai rushed to add, "I see the stubborn upon him, but the way he watches you and waits, he will come around probably sooner than seems logical."

"Thank you, Jaliqai," I said. "I do prefer the raw honesty," I added to them both. But I felt the need to direct things away from my worry. That Thalaj would come around was all I could hope for, but discussing it wouldn't bring his acceptance about any sooner. I'd caused the conflict by the time I had spent with Sarangarel, but I would never trade that experience, and what passed between us was private—something I'd never share with my guard and protector in word or deed. It had opened new possibilities to me and bloomed curiosity. In its own right, it held a beauty I couldn't have fathomed, nor could I explain it in words. However, it did make me wonder at the nature of relations and relationships between the Stone Singers in a more general sense. Looking between the two women beside me, I decided I'd ask when the time felt right and turned my attention to learning more about these people. My people still. "Yisu? Will you tell me about this title?"

With one last look, I turned my back on Nantai and the City by the Sea, and as we strode around the deck, Jaliqai started, "*Yisun* is an ancient term. In Nantai, it means *nine.*"

"*The* nine," Chambui interjected. "The number nine is very lucky to our people."

"But there are only five of you," I objected.

Jaliqai chuckled. "There are nine, but the others remained with Gnoble Sarangarel for reasons threefold. The others have littles right now, and that is a rare gift they wouldn't leave unless it were a matter of life and death. Secondly, our peoples' leader never lets us all go on a mission together. There must always be someone to train others should we not return."

Silence fell for several minutes until I asked, "You mentioned a third?"

"Communication," Chambui said shortly.

I halted in my tracks, sucking in a sharp breath. "Communication? Across the Syrensea? How is that possible?"

Chambui clasped my hand in hers. "Kōgō Evangale, our Lady Sarangarel has said that we may trust you. Our men are skeptical." She looked down at our joined hands.

Jaliqai looked around as if wanting to make certain no one listened in on our conversation. "We are putting a lot of trust in you by sharing this secret. We ask that you keep it in confidence."

I nodded. "Of course."

Chambui squeezed my hand. "Even from your shadow."

My shadow. The label seemed fitting, yet aside from the Sarangarel and her Stone Singers, no one had called him that before. "Understood." I swallowed. "And . . . I will."

Jaliqai produced a blood-red stone, opaque as the night, from a pouch she wore around her waist. She held it in cupped hands so that only I could see, then tucked it back into her purse as quickly as possible. "It's the rarest gem we know. And our people have had them since before the first age. Stone Singers call it *yarikhgüi yarikh*, which literally translates to 'speak no speak,' but in Nantai, we simply say 'talking stone.' To our knowledge, there are only nine. One each in the custody of a yisun."

The other yisu urged us along. "Enough of that. Just so you know, we can use them if needed." Chambui grinned. "So let's talk of lighter things. The journey is long."

I learned a little about the lives of the Stone Singers that morning, that their lifespans were almost double that of the rest of the castes of Nantai. They weren't certain why, but their teachings said it had something to do with their connection to Mother Earth herself. The way they spoke of it, it seemed almost as if they worshipped her rather than the Triad, but I left that questioning for another day.

About their relationships, Chambui said, "It is almost impossible for us to mate with a singular person for so long. Everyone changes over time, so we dispelled the notion of monogamy long, long ago. The only time we settle is in the time we breed and raise littles. That is often enough for people to grow, change, and ready themselves for the next stage in their lives. Maybe it is another breeding cycle or maybe something different altogether."

The concept confounded me but seemed logical as they presented the notion. Given the Stone Singers' longevity, I inquired about Sarangarel's age. She'd looked older than me, but only by a matter of seasons, not decades. They both flinched, but in the end, Jaliqai said straightly,

"She's just entered her second age."

My jaw hung. "You mean she's passed four hundred seasons?" That alone was longer than any Storm Sorcerer could hope to live.

The women both smiled and raised their brows in mirror images.

Jaliqai added, "Our bodies don't age until our last twenty or so seasons; the decline is quick. By the time we show our age, we are typically nearing our third age."

"Though," Chambui said, "there are those among us who have lived into a third age without showing the signs."

I strolled, in awe by the manner in which they revealed the knowledge of their people. They seemed to know more of the other castes, Storm Sorcerers included, than we knew of them, and I internally cursed our method of learning and bonding as a nation . . . heavy books penned by the first caste and handed down by decree from ruler to ruler. Each emperor or empress held so little knowledge about the world beyond Arashi and the High Cloud Courts. I wondered what facts they'd omitted from the histories with intent throughout the ages. It'd also been the Triad's duty to bless each and every book before it found its way into the library at Stormskeep. Had they had a hand in censoring information as well?

Certainly, the Storm Sorcerers believed it was a means of sharing knowledge—I had to believe that much of my caste and kin—but could they not have listened and observed first?

That I had never learned these basic details of a people I also called my own due to this inadequate practice angered me. If I were to ever repeat my ascension, I would decree changes to this tradition, that we would welcome those from other castes into our city to maintain histories of all our folk. Or mayhap we would allow them to pen their own and share them across the land. Perhaps by my decree, we could erase the notion of castes entirely. I sighed at the thought, doubtful that such a day would come. Yet one could hope.

I vowed then and there that when I restored my father to the throne, I would request these things of him before I took my leave. The small taste I'd had of other ways of life had whetted my appetite. I wanted to travel to the farthest corners of the world, meet as many people as possible, and learn their ways. The thought of sitting on a cold throne soured my stomach. Something had bored its way into my skin and bones, and I felt that seedling sprouting into an overwhelming desire to experience whatever this journey to find Father held and much, much more.

Over the next days, I came to know Yisu Chambui and Yisu Jaliqai better, and I had several occasions to witness the freedom of which they had spoken that first morning upon the *Swell Mistress*. The days were long in the hot season, and throughout every day and night, it seemed that Thalaj would avoid me as long as possible. I tried to take comfort in the things about him others had witnessed—that he would return to me time and time again, that jealousy angered him, that he watched from afar and tried to balance his ire with us still being there together . . . yet he still seemed reluctant.

One night, it remained light as we just finished the day's last meal. My party save Thalaj gathered around the large table above deck, Hoaris with his cup and dice.

Yisun Baidu dumped a large pile of gems upon the table that we'd use as currency for the betting. There were colors aplenty, and we each gathered the color of our choice. Mine were a deep amethyst, so dark purple they barely caught the light within their facets. Others were red, blue, orange, green, and almost any other color one could imagine. Baidu put away the leftovers and we diced for an hour or more, laughing as we passed stones to the right when we rolled a four, to the left when we rolled a five, and put it in the pot when we rolled a six. Everyone would blow on the dice for luck and hope to roll low numbers. When someone won the pot, they seized the pile of rainbow-colored stones in the center of the table.

On we played. The game remained friendly, and when someone ran out of stones, the others would return their color and we'd begin another game.

Just as Otarr sank in the sky, Captain Asahi arrived with a wooden cask under one arm and a lantern in the other.

Misha issued a peal of high-pitched laughter while he and Kyr dug into their purses. "Put that out." The small woman waved a hand at the lantern. "Things can get dangerous over dice. I'd hate to burn the ship."

Kyr placed four stones on the long table and set them to glow with a quick word. The captain gave a satisfied nod and extinguished the lantern in favor of the safer lights. He grabbed some metal cups and filled each from his cask, passing them around as he did. When I sipped, it burned a streak down my throat and a fiery shiver erupted from my stomach shaking my entire body.

"Whoa," I breathed as if trying to expel the fire from my throat.

Asahi dropped a hand on my back. "Take another. It gets better." He walked around the table. "May I join ya?"

A series of rumbles and cheers went up, and I tasted

again. He was right; the warmth in my throat was nice the second time around, and even nicer with every drink following.

The dicing and drinking went on well into the night. At one point, I lamented for my trusted protector, but I tried hard to keep those thoughts at bay.

Selene was a sliver that night in the sky, and the stars were brighter than I'd ever seen. They swam in the darkness above as the ship rocked gently on the sea's waves beneath me. The combination was dizzying.

"They are pretty, lovely," Kyr said, pushing one of the lighted stones closer. "But you'll wanna keep level. Keep your eyes on this. That's good. You'll feel better that way."

We played some more. Laughter rang through the night and roared around the deck. It was the wildest night and time I could recall until people calmed and drifted toward sleep. While Jaliqai had retired with Timur the prior evening, she presently cuddled at the end of the table with another of the yisun, Nachin. The same was true with Chambui. She'd spent last evening with Nachin, but showed favor for Baidu.

This went on for a while, and I glanced at Timur. It appeared he'd be the lone man out that evening.

Seeing my glance, he gave a crooked smile and a half-laugh. "No worries about me. That one"—he nodded toward Jaliqai—"wore me out last night. I'll be in for a good sleep after this drink." He polished off the last of it and stood, holding onto the rail and still weaving as he made his way to the center of the ship where he could climb down to the private cabins.

I bit the inside of my lip, worrying if I'd be able to make that journey on my own. I watched after him and tried to plan my steps for some time. The laughter died out, and others retired for the night.

"Do you need some help there, Mairy?" Hoaris boomed.

I stared at the man's beard, red though I knew it was, it seemed dark gray in the night. *Fascinating*, I thought. Then, a pale hand from nowhere rested on his shoulder and a soft familiar voice said, "I have this, old friend."

Hoaris stood and left by way of the railing.

I looked up. He slipped out of the night's shadow, and I held his almond-shaped eyes with my own gaze as he sat across the table.

My eyes prickled as I breathed, "Thalaj?"

Dramatis Personae

Storm Sorcerers

Evangales and family

Atheryn Evangale—Tennō of Nantai; father to Karynne, Mairynne, and Yasmynne

Corwyn Dawnsgale—Nadia's consort, Solarynne's brother

Karynne "Kahry" Evangale—first daughter to Atheryn and Noralynne; Mairynne and Yasmynne's sister.

Mairynne Evangale—Lady Mairynne; third daughter to Atheryn and Noralynne

Nadialynne "Nadia" Riversgale—Noralynne's twin sister, aunt to Karynne, Mairynne, and Yasmynne

Noralynne Evangale—Kōgō of Nantai; empress; Atheryn's wife; mother to Karynne, Mairynne, and Yasmynne

Kōgō Phelyse—empress in the Second Age, second ruler of that age

Yasmynne Evangale—sister to Mairynne and Karynne; betrothed to Nestryn

First Advisors

Imrythel Sandsgale—Karynne's first advisor

Nestryn—Yasmynne's betrothed and first advisor

Clergy (raised to serve the Triad)

Arlyn Hallowgale—Priest of Otarr, the sun god/the Day-Seer

Baldwyn—Acolyte of Otarr, the sun god /the Day-Seer

Edamyn Hallowgale—Priest of Atun, the all-seeing god / the All-Seer; oldest priest

Tasmynne Hallowgale—Priestess of Selene, the moon goddess/the Night-Seer

Counselors

Azurynne Nightingale—matriarch of the Nightingale family

Lukosyn "Lukos" Thundergale—patriarch of the Thundergale family

Ohmyn Havengale—patriarch of the Havengale family

Solarynne Dawnsgale—Corwyn's sister, matriarch of the Dawnsgale family

Guards

Gaelynne

Roryn Seagale

Perryn

Tarlyn—leads the Arashi guard in Thalaj's absence

Thalaj Northerngale—Gensui of Nantai's Arashi guard

Other

Dorynne—Mairynne's attendant

Idalynne "Mother" Feathergale—nanny to Karynne, Mairynne, and Yasmynne

Jessamynne "Jessa" Feathergale—Idalynne's daughter, friend to Mairynne

Larynne—Nadia's handmaid

Makenyn the Scarred—First Emperor of Nantai

Morwyn—Makenyn's brother

Nityn—Shaman who banished the dragon from Makenyn

Sentei **Summergale**—healer in Arashi

Teralynne - Healer apprentice

Zafrynne Keeningale—Witch woman/spellcaster

Deities (named) & Holy Triad

Holy Triad

Atun (aka the All-Seer)—Nantai God, part of the Holy Triad the all-seeing god; father to Otarr and Selene

Otarr (aka the Day-Seer)—Nantai God, part of the Holy Triad, associated with the sun; Atun's child; the sun god

Selene (aka the Night-Seer) —Nantai Goddess, part of the Triad, associated with the moon; Atun's daughter; the moon goddess

Ryū (Dragons, Ryū dragons, dragons)

Kuroidragon (Kuroi), black dragon, bonded with Makenyn

Barūdragon (Barū), blue dragon

Cloud Courtiers

Alto-Raal

Alto-Trea—The Swan, Filtch

Cirro-Tsan—Comtess Tsanseri, Comtesse of the Masque; Lady of Masks

Cirro-Vior "Viordyn" —crescent moon shape on the shoulder; used to be a childhood friend of Mairynne's

Strato-Ymar—Gnoble of the caste

Fire Forgers

Yuos Atith—Gnoble of the caste

Frost Fighters (of the fourth caste)

Aljir Tenkara—Gnoble of the caste

Stone Singers

Sarangarel—Gnoble of the caste (female)

The Yisun

Baidu, yisun (male)

Chambui, yisu (female)

Jaliqai, yisu (female)

Timir, yisun (male)

Nachin, yisun (male)

Underhill Dwellers

Brimr—Gnoble of the caste

Svarta—Brimr's wife

Casteless

"street rats"

Honera

Flea

Gnat

Jerek, Captain of the river barge

Sal, Inkeeper in Safaia

Wren

Sailors

Asahi, Captain of the Swell Mistress

Small Folk

(of Umbra and Brennmor)

Isao, King of the small folk / The Small King

Kyr, Misha's partner

Misha, third son of royalty, Kyr's partner of choice

Tsinti

nomadic people, "Nantai wanderers of the grasslands"

Baldeo

Beltrana, new baby

Buharro

Detsa

Gashparis, new baby

Janci, Yankos's son

Jorani (called Miss Firefly by Kyr of the Small Folk)

Maladros

Mizo, new baby

Yankos, currently represents Tsinti people at parliament every seventh year, but doesn't call himself a leader (says all are equal)

Zofi, witch woman/spellcaster

ACKNOWLEDGEMENTS

I'D LIKE TO THANK the people who supported me while I wrote this series as well as the people who read and provided feedback on Mairynne's story. It was a couple of years in the making, and you have all been saviors in helping this project see the light of day.

To my husband, Reno, thank you for giving me space and time to write, edit, plan to release, market, and publish this work.

To Mackenzie, Keeton, Ian, Paige, Lisa, Jake, and the entire Kuhn family, thank you for reading the drafts and providing valuable feedback to better the story.

To Ursula, thank you for being the most patient editor in the world.

ABOUT THE AUTHOR

SUSAN STRADIOTTO WRITES FANTASY for New Adult audiences and later Young Adult audiences, with storylines enjoyable for adults too. Themes focus mostly on relationships of all kinds, family situations, coming of age, and finding oneself or ones destiny.

She lives in Eden Prairie, Minnesota with her husband, two of her three children, and two fur children. She has worked in Technology for more years than she'd like to admit, but storytelling is her true passion. She has always been a voracious reader, lover of worlds, and a "werd nerd." Susan's infatuation with well-developed characters sometimes rivals her relationships with real people.

Susan fills her own soul by spending her free time writing, networking with other writers, and occasionally camping "up-north." If you're from Minnesota, you'll get the reference along with "hot dish" and "grey-duck." If you're not from Minnesota, you probably don't want to ask. Note that she's originally a Texan, and that never leaves you.

CONNECT ON SOCIAL MEDIA

https://www.goodreads.com/susanstradiotto

https://www.instagram.com/susanstradiotto/

https://www.facebook.com/susanstradiottoauthor/

https://twitter.com/StradiottoS

https://www.bookbub.com/authors/susan-stradiotto

CPSIA information can be obtained
at www.ICGtesting.com
Printed in the USA
LVHW022126260421
685610LV00017B/771

9 781949 357202